UNDER THE RED
OAK TREE

∽ J.M. VIERSTRA ∽

ISBN 978-1-64079-771-0 (paperback)
ISBN 978-1-64079-772-7 (digital)

Christian Faith Publishing, Inc.
832 Park Avenue
Meadville, PA 16335
www.christianfaithpublishing.com

Printed in the United States of America

In loving memory of Michael G. Vierstra

Chapter 1

"GRANDPA, GRANDPA!" YELLED LITTLE FAITH as we pulled into my father's driveway. She had a distinct sound of excitement when she knew she was going to get to spend some time with grandpa. I definitely get excited to see dad too. He is a very kind and compassionate man that has been through the mill and back. He loves the girls and I love that they share a strong relationship together. He has been a positive part of my life as long as I can remember. That has played a huge part in how I act as a father.

My chest started to tighten the closer we got to the house. I was excited to talk with him and get my mind off all the stress at work. Life seemed to be full of constant, unending problems and I could swear at every corner a new problem would present itself. It felt like it was just one after another. At least I had a family to stand by my side and give me their encouragement. That by itself is a priceless blessing from God.

I tended to think about God often throughout my life. I think it is part of being raised in a Christian home. The Bible has taught me so much on how to live my life. It taught me about mercy, kindness, compassion, and so many other positive traits. My favorite of those is love. Love is powerful. It was strong enough to give me and my sister a family when we lost our own.

Our biological father passed away before I was born and our biological mother died giving birth to me. My sister and I were both so young we don't remember them but from my research, they were both good people. In the end, God's plan was perfect because it sent us the parents I grew up with.

I pulled my truck up next to dad's simple white house. The twins were so excited to get inside I could barely manage to get them out of their seatbelts. I unbuckled Faith and she took off inside before I had the chance to get Hope out. Hope was the calmer of the two. I gently helped her out of her booster seat and set her on the ground. She was getting ready to bolt up the walkway and get inside, but she became distracted.

She slowly walked over to some yellow flowers planted by the side of the house. She squatted down and reached her innocent, loving hand toward a butterfly resting on a flower. It was absolutely precious watching her become captivated by God's creation. Just when she was about to touch the butterfly, it took off into the sky. Hope jumped back from being startled as it fluttered from the flower's petals. I let out a soft laugh under my breath. She had a look of shock on her face as she turned toward me. Then she smiled and started laughing as she took off into the house.

I started thinking about how peaceful children are. The elderly too. They both seem to be the most gracious and appreciative of people. The people that seem to have the most problems are the middle-aged. Most of them seem to be worried about how much money they make or their social status. I have seen people work away their lives getting a fortune saved up just to die of an accident. It's tragic—not just the accident or the pre-mature loss of life, but the misuse of it. Life is a gift from God. It is valuable and should be used to love Him and each other. We all have our bumps in the road but that's why scripture says, "Being reasonably happy in this world and supremely happy in the next."

I turned back toward the truck so I could help my wife carry in the groceries. Kelli already had the bag of groceries in her hand and was walking toward me.

"Do you want me to carry those in?" I asked.

"No, I can carry them." Kelli responded.

She walked by me and gave me a gentle smile. I loved her more than love itself. She is hands down the greatest wife a husband could ask for. I loved her from the moment I looked into her bright blue eyes. She was beyond beautiful, starting from her core. I had never met a woman that could take my breath away like she did.

I walked into dad's house and he was in the kitchen with the twins. He was dishing out three bowls of vanilla ice cream for the twins and him. That seemed to be their thing. Every time we stopped by Grandpa Luke's house, they would twist his arm for ice cream. I didn't mind them sharing the treat because they bonded so well together.

"Happy birthday!" I mildly yelled as I stepped into the kitchen.

"Thanks." He replied.

"You're not going to wait till after dinner for some ice cream?" I asked.

He responded with a smirk, "Nah, this year I decided we will have dessert early." The twins didn't object, they just looked up at me and smiled with ice cream dripping down their chins.

I looked my dad over and he seemed to be having one of his better days. It amazed me that he was turning ninety years old. He looked so good for his age but the years have taken their toll. I could tell he felt weak even though he tried to show strength. I didn't like to think about his battle with lung cancer. He has been fighting for three tough years and I feared it was his last. I wasn't afraid of him dying because he was right with the Lord, but I was afraid of living without him. I have never experienced a day without him being part of my life and didn't like the idea of that happening. I loved him too much to say goodbye.

I would say watching him fight to breathe was one of the toughest struggles I had ever been through. I felt helpless because all I could do to help was be supportive. I couldn't take the cancer from him and I had to trust God's plan. I didn't feel it was supposed to be like this. He is my father and, tough as nails. I have seen him pull splinters from his bare hand and never wince, but cancer was a completely different battle. It hit him like a freight train but how he reacted was inspirational. He embraced it because he had an endless faith that he was in God's hands. It changed my perspective of how I felt about death. It helped me understand it is the beginning, not the end.

I started to think of some of my memories of dad. They made me feel simultaneously happy and sad. Happy because they reminded me of how great of a person he is but sad because I wouldn't be able to make many more with him.

My thinking got sidetracked as I heard tires pushing on the gravel driveway. Faith and Hope took off toward the living room. Their blond hair was bouncing up and down with their bodies as they ran and all I could do was smile. They got to the window in the living room and looked outside.

"Aunty Kate!" They yelled in unison.

I headed out the door so I could help bring in the cooking. My older sister Kate loved to cook and she always made dinner for dad's birthday. I got out to her car and grabbed a pot of mashed potatoes.

"I knew you were good for something," Kate said with a cynical tone. She gave me a smile and embraced me in her arms as I stood there holding the pot.

"That's why they pay me the big bucks," I said as I smiled back.

She grabbed a bottle of wine and said, "Don't take too long. We're all starving." She took off inside before I had a chance to respond. That little rascal didn't come back to help either. I hauled in all the food as Kelli was setting the table. My sister had a glass of red wine in her hand and walked in to the dining room to help Kelli set up.

"So brother, how's work at the mill going?" Kate asked.

"It's just as busy as always. People still need lumber."

The mill had turned into quite the prestigious business around our town. Dad started it when I was little and I started running it when he retired. I enjoyed the business because of the flexible hours, but the downside was the mill was constantly running. It was easy to get an hour off, but not a day. We were about to open our first retail lumber store too, so my workload would increase significantly with that around the corner.

Dad walked into the room and sat down for dinner. Kelli gathered up the girls and we all sat together as a family. Kate's husband couldn't make it this time because he worked long hours at the hospital but nevertheless, most of us were there.

Dad started dinner off traditionally, with prayer.

"Let us pray," he said.

We all bowed our heads and closed our eyes. Even the girls were adamant about taking prayer seriously.

"Lord, thank you for this pleasant year that we have all been blessed with. Some may take the gift of time for granted but we are truly thankful. Thank you for this meal and may it nourish our bodies and produce strength. I ask that you make this birthday very special. In Jesus's name I pray, Amen."

We all enjoyed the delicious meal in front of us. We were passing plates around with an abundance of food. The girls loved Aunty Kate's cooking. I was rather fond of it as well. It was a very nice dinner, with great conversation and a strong family presence.

After dinner, the ladies picked up the plates and proceeded on with washing up the dishes. I joined dad in the living room where he was playing with the girls. They were rolling a ball over the carpet from one to another.

As I walked in, dad sat up on the couch and said, "If I could change one thing about my life, it would be to spend more time with you kids. I spent all my time after prison catching up with what I missed out. Now, I realize I had everything I ever needed. I just looked past it. If you want my advice, I would say stay content with maintaining the business. The desire for growth should never compromise the time your family needs with you."

It put a smile on my face with the truth of his statement. I simply replied with a nod.

"And son, I have been doing a lot of thinking about this. Next time you hire an employee, I want you to do this. Think of it as an experiment and let me know what happens. The next time you hire someone and they come for their first day of work. I want you to turn them around and send them home for the day. I want you to tell them that their first job is to be a husband and a father. That is if they are a husband or father. If they are neither, then tell them to spend it with a parent or sibling and if they have no one, then invite him to spend the day with you. Tell them that you want them to really spend that time with family because they come before work. You could teach a man a good life lesson that way."

I smiled back at him and knew he was serious about helping people.

"It is important that your employees have good values and their priorities are in line."

I nodded in agreement. Dad always tried to teach me life lessons like that when I was a kid. He showed me honesty and integrity rather than only tell me about it. I remember all the small things he did, like holding the door open or just the simple courtesy he showed others. He was my role model growing up and he still is to this day. It's hard for me to understand how a man that everyone idolizes still has so much humility. Most of the time pride grows in a man the more he is idolized. It was different for dad.

I think the difference was he made the conscious choice to make himself lesser than others. In his own mind he believed everyone was more important than himself. I thought of him as a better person than most, but he took himself off that pedestal a long time ago. It was hard to contemplate that growing up.

He would say to me in my youth, "Last place is only bad when it is the position you don't want to finish. It's about perception. Your perception is your reality."

I never really understood it until I got older. I knew people loved champions and I wanted to be one of those champions. I wanted people to look up to me and be proud of me, but dad was never like that. He didn't search for fulfillment in other people and by doing so, people looked up to him. I know I did and so did my mom.

I think his contentment was one of the parts my mom loved most about him. He found his identity in Christ and needed nothing else. I turned and looked at the side table next to the couch. There was a picture of him and mom together. They looked so happy together. Dad had definitely aged though. He was still tall but his hair had whitened and his face had aged.

I stared at my mom in the picture. In the picture, it looked like they were at a lake somewhere. Mom was wearing a yellow baseball cap with her brunette hair in a ponytail. I stared into her brown eyes as I thought about how much I missed her. She was a beautiful lady inside and out. We lost her over a decade ago because of complications with her heart. My theory is her heart was supposed to be made of flesh but hers was made of gold.

Kate and Kelli walked in after they finished up the dishes. Everyone sat down around the living room when dad started to speak.

"This year is a special year for me. I want to tell as much of my life story as I can remember. Most importantly, I want to tell you how God was always there for me. In my entire lifetime, He never left me, even when my life was at rock bottom. It is time I finally tell you about my walk through misery. I want you to really focus on the morality of what I was taught through my tribulations and how God can turn trial into triumph."

Chapter 2

I T WAS THE MIDDLE OF November. A light layer of snow barely covered the ground from the early morning frost. I could feel the damp, cool air on my face and my hands were already starting to feel like ice under my gloves. Most mornings started like this. It was all part of the job. I was nineteen years old working full time hauling logs for the mill. I loved my job. I would even say I lived for my job. I was on the fast track to success, hard work. I was never shy about putting in more hours than everyone around me. I loved the idea of luxury and that was the only way I knew I could obtain it.

I headed to my old, white logging truck. I sat in the seat and turned the key so the cool diesel engine could warm. It took a second to get it started. As it started, dark charcoal smoke erupted out of the tailpipe. Every time I pushed on the petal, the cloud of smoke only grew.

I walked back to my car to get my daily supplies. Everything was in place. I had my straps, pocket knife, and thermos full of hot coffee. I was the type of person that liked to be prepared so I usually packed heavy. After I felt I was ready, I hopped into my logging truck and headed off to the job site.

One of my favorite parts of the job was the view. The countryside was beautiful. The light layer of snow was already beginning to melt as the temperature rose. The leaves on the trees were a beautiful mixture of color. The sun was bright and very few clouds crossed the sky. I loved every moment. Everything I saw was pleasant, from the wild life to wild flowers. In my mind, it was perfection.

I reached the road that led to the log site. I could hear the tires of my truck push against the gravel road. It was only a couple more minutes before I could get my first load of the day. I looked up the hill side and saw some deer hopping through the woods. They were peaceful and pleasant to watch. My soul was satisfied. My body was too from the eggs and potatoes I had for breakfast.

As I pulled into the loading site, I saw the boss man directing the truck in front of me. How fast they could load our trucks was an art. Before I knew it, they had mine loaded too. They had it filled to the brim and they strapped all the logs down to the bed. I was ready to go so I headed to the mill to drop off my first load of the day.

Everything was a typical day until I looked in my rearview mirror and saw the strap that was supposed to keep the logs held down fluttering in the wind. I pulled into a turn off by the side of the road. It was a landmark to the locals because of the giant oak tree that sat only a few yards from the road. The tree was massive and well-known because of the unique way the branches grew and twisted.

I turned off the truck and jumped out to see what had happened. I walked over to the strap and somehow it had broken. My only theory was it had come loose and broke against the ground. At least it didn't get tangled in my axle because that would have caused another set of problems. "Easy fix," I thought.

I kept some spare rope under the seat of my truck that I could use to tie everything together. I pulled the strap back over the logs. I tugged and pulled as hard as I could. Once it seemed tight enough I used my spare rope to fasten it down to the truck bed. I had it tied down to the best of my ability. There was a long tail of excess rope that I didn't want to come loose so I decided to cut it. I pulled out my pocket knife and started to cut.

The knife I had was a dull piece of junk. I kept putting more and more pressure on it as I tried to get through the rope. I was pushing and ripping when suddenly, I went straight through it. I instantly knew something was wrong. I felt a jolt of heat shoot up my arm and I started to sweat.

I looked down and felt the discomfort in my hand. Everything seemed to move in slow motion. As my eyes reached my hand, I saw blood barely moving out of the large gash in my palm. It was like water slowly drizzling out the end of a hose. I didn't have a lot of thoughts going through my head. The only emotion I felt was disbelief.

Time rushed back to its original pace. Blood started gushing from the slit in my hand and I instantly felt lightheaded when I saw it. I stumbled back and leaned against the oak tree. I waited until I regained my balance and took deep breaths. I couldn't believe everything happened so quickly. One moment it was a typical day at work, the next I was severely injured for the first time in my life.

I managed to pull my tee shirt off and wrapped it around my hand to slow the bleeding. I didn't feel a lot of pain but there was a lot of blood. I elevated my hand and blood dripped down my forearm onto the ground. I decided to reevaluate the situation and see how bad it was. I pulled the shirt back so I could get a better look.

It was deep and I could see the flesh pulled apart. The wound had reached my bone. Then there was an instant, searing pain. It felt like my mind told it to start hurting. I knew I needed to go to a doctor so I got back in the truck and headed to town. It seemed like a lifetime getting out of the countryside. I no longer cared about the views or work. My only focus was on my hand.

It didn't take long to get back into town. The most difficult part was driving the truck with one hand. I put my wounded hand under my leg and used the pressure to slow the bleeding. It worked for the most part but there was still going to be a mess.

I actually felt proud for the way I handled the situation. I didn't panic or react harshly. I simply focused on the problem and headed to the solution. I pulled into the hospital parking lot and found a place in the back to park. I walked inside and they had me stitched up quickly. The doctor commented that it was a clean cut so the scar wouldn't be very large. I didn't really care about that, I was just happy because it could have been worse.

The slice went clear across the front of my left hand and it was very tender. I knew I was going to have to take a couple days off work. I informed my boss and he told me to, "Get healed up and get back out here." I learned I better be more careful when I'm out in the wilderness. Things change on a dime.

When I got home, my mood changed to depressed and angry. I couldn't believe I made such a stupid mistake. *Why did I make such a stupid decision?* I thought. I was out of work, my hand hurt like crazy, and to top it all off, I ruined my tee shirt. I spent the rest of my day hanging around the house by myself. I worked hard for independence but at that point I could have used some company. I was frustrated so I laid down on the living room couch to try to relax.

I stared at the blank ceiling as I felt sorry for myself. My blood was boiling at that point. I knew better then to make a petty mistake but I never thought anything bad would happen to me.

I continued to stare at the white paint on my ceiling until in a split second I dozed off. I woke up to a pounding on the door. I figured my mom caught wind of me being hurt and was coming to check on me. I was still curious as to who it could be though because I didn't tell anyone besides my boss.

I moved the curtain and glanced outside the window, it was a police officer. *What could he possibly want?* I thought. I sat up and walked toward the door. I felt lightheaded from standing so suddenly. I stood there for a second and regained clarity before I reached for the doorknob. I grabbed it and pulled the door open.

The officer was a large man with a badge over his heart and the name Stone on his uniform. I looked him up and down as he did the same to me. He was about my height and that was unusual because most weren't as tall as me. He wasn't wearing a hat but had a full head of brown hair. He had a deep voice and broad shoulders but at the same time seemed friendly.

"Mr. Luke Cassidy?" he asked. I nodded to show it was me.

"Luke, I need to ask you some questions." He stated blatantly.

"Okay?" I replied with a curious look on my face.

"I will get right to the point. We are investigating a homicide and medical records showed you were in the hospital for a knife wound that occurred yesterday. Can you tell me how you injured your hand?"

My face instantly turned pale, but not from any sort of guilt. It was from pure shock and disbelief. I knew nothing about anyone dying. I stood in the entryway and told him what happened with my hand. I told him it was an accident that happened while cutting rope.

"I believe you but I need you to come down to the station and make a statement." "What? Why? I told you everything I know," I replied.

"Well that's confidential, Mr. Cassidy. Just come to the station and I will explain."

I sighed and decided it would be best to go there and figure everything out. I started thinking to myself, *Why would the police care I hurt my hand"* It had nothing to do with me and I was very mad about the inconvenience.

"Who was killed?" I asked as we walked toward the road.

"Jean Cooper was found out in the woods. We found her body after she was reported missing last night."

I was even more shocked. It was a small town so everybody at least knew of each other. I didn't really know the girl but I knew who she was. It was overwhelmed me for a murder to occur in general.

"She was the mayor's daughter right? I don't even know the girl. I have talked to her maybe once or twice, but she is a couple years younger than me."

"I know, son, this is all procedure for an investigation. Once we get down to the station then we will get this all straightened out."

I was walking toward my car when Officer Stone stopped me. He told me that I had to ride in the back of the cop car and wear handcuffs. I complied because I didn't want to cause any problems. I hated the dreadful click the handcuffs made as he tightened the cool steel around my wrists. They were definitely not designed for comfort.

Getting into the back of the cop car was a different experience all on its own. I had never been in the back of a cop car before. In fact, I had never been in any trouble my entire life. I had to duck my head to fit in the back. The officer helped but by no means was it comfortable. I don't know what to call the emotion I was feeling because it was new to me. It wasn't shame because I hadn't done anything wrong, but it was along those lines because I was still in an awful situation.

After I was in and was situated, he closed the door and sat in the driver's seat. The handcuffs really started to dig into my skin after about a minute. It was painful because I couldn't do much to get them resituated. I could only move them slightly up and down, and avoid putting any pressure on them. It hardly helped and that caused me to become even more irritated.

I looked up and said harshly, "Why do I have to ride in here anyway?"

"It's the way it works when you're a suspect." He responded.

Suspect? I thought to myself. *Why am I a suspect? How could this be real?* I spent the entire ride to the station waiting to wake up. I figured at any moment my eyes would open and I would stare right back up at the ceiling. That was when the waiting, the constant waiting, started.

Chapter 3

I WILL ALWAYS REMEMBER GETTING out of the cop car. I looked out and saw two men in suits standing side by side. They were at the top of the steps by the entrance of the police station. I was escorted out of the car and walked into the station with the officer holding the top of my arm.

"Is this really necessary?" I asked a little rudely.

He didn't respond. He simply continued to bring me inside the police station. Then they put me into a small room and sat me down in a chair. I started to ask if he would take off the handcuffs but he bolted out of the door once I opened my mouth. I sat there looking around. The room was bland, all white walls with a brown wood desk and a few chairs. The entire room was only about two arm lengths wide.

I pinched the outside of my leg and it didn't feel good. I realized that I wasn't going to wake up. I was in reality and I was really at the police station. It was officially the worst day ever. After a while one of the men in a suit stepped in.

He was a tall slender man that stood with a strong posture. He walked in and sat down in a chair across from me. I stared at his wide nose as he sniffed and wiped it with his hand. He had a full brown mustache and a little stubble starting to grow on the rest of his face. On top, he was bald besides the short brown hair that wrapped around the side of his head.

"Mr. Luke Cassidy?" He asked.

"Yes," I replied.

"I'm Detective Evans and I'm here investigating a murder. Before I get started, I would like to inform you of your rights." He read them to me and asked if I understood them clearly.

I responded, "Yes," then he started to interrogate me.

"Can you tell me what you have been up to over the last couple days?"

I responded defensively. I didn't want to answer his questions. I didn't want to be there at all. I'm sure I came out a little rude when I responded.

"Sir, I don't know what's going on but I didn't hurt anyone."

"Well, how did you hurt your hand?" He asked.

"I cut my hand working. It was an accident."

"So… you're a liar," he said.

"What? No, how am I a liar?"

"You just said that you never hurt anyone," he responded.

"I didn't hurt anyone," I responded defensively.

"Well, you claim to have hurt yourself. That falls into the category as anyone and that makes you a liar."

"That's not what I meant," I responded.

"Well, Mr. Cassidy, now I assume that you are a dishonest man. Let's make this simple. I know that you murdered Miss Cooper."

I felt a drop of sweat run down my forehead and my heart was pounding so hard I felt like I was going to go into cardiac arrest. I felt heat rush throughout my body and I could feel my face turn red. My palms started dripping sweat and the wrap around my hand started to moisten.

I was terrified, definitely the most scared I had ever been my entire life. I never had anyone look me in the eye as if I was a monster before. That was an out of body experience all by itself.

I barely managed to sputter out, "No, that isn't true. I did not, this can't be real." He stood up and stepped out of the room without saying another word, but had this unique look like I was the worst person in the world. His stare intimidated me to the fullest.

A moment later, the other man in the suit walked in. He was a short, fat guy that was bald as could be. He walked in and sat down just as the detective before him. He was already breathing hard as he sat down. It made me feel more uncomfortable because I didn't want to be around him. Then he grinned slightly and I could see the large gap in the middle of his teeth. He looked up into my eyes and spoke.

"I'm the District Attorney, Mr. Green, and I want to help you."

His voice had an odd squeak in it. It was subtle and seemed like an accent, but not one I had ever heard before. All I knew was I was uncomfortable and irritated.

"I didn't do anything. You have the wrong guy," I replied.

"Well, the evidence gathered so far points to you as the perpetrator. If you just admit to what you did, the judge will look very favorably on that. I have the ability to get you a fair plea deal, all you have to do is confess and then we can help you."

Suddenly Evans swung open the door. I jumped back startled as he yelled, "You're going to die in prison for what you did!"

I didn't know what to do or think at that moment. Everything was turning into a blur and I felt sick to my stomach. I couldn't think properly. *Why wouldn't they listen?* If I didn't tell them what they wanted to hear, then they didn't respond to it. All they wanted was to get me to confess and it was something I had nothing to do with. It was like they didn't care what the truth was. They just wanted a confession.

The questions kept coming left and right. They almost felt like punches. I told them the truth. I figured as long as I stayed honest everything would work out. I told them about my hand slipping while I was cutting the rope.

They snarled back, "Lies! We do this for a living. We know you are lying."

Hours and hours went by, one would walk in and tell me I was a murderer and he was going to ensure I would never walk free again. Then a few minutes, later the prosecutor would come in and say, "We can still help you if you're accountable for your actions. You probably won't get a life sentence."

I didn't take comfort in that statement at all. Serving even a moment of time would be a complete injustice. I couldn't comprehend their line of thinking. *How could they think this is okay?* The lashes they were taking at me became too much to tolerate.

I became nauseated and couldn't take it anymore. I wanted it to end. I wanted to go home. I had never been in any trouble and I didn't deserve what was going on. I was an honest man. I rarely ever lied and when I did, it was to protect someone I cared about. I couldn't lie about something this big. I couldn't have lived with myself. I was sick of the pressure and yelling. I decided it would be best to call for help. I decided to call my mother and see what she had to say. I was scared to ask but I decided it was time to be strong. I had to get tough and handle the situation.

I stood up and told them I would like to call my mother. The detective stood up across from me with his chest puffed out and said, "You're not going anywhere." He stepped toward me and told me to turn around and put my hands behind my back.

"You're under arrest for the murder of Jean Cooper."

I instantly started to cry with all the emotion running through my veins. They consisted of hurt, disbelief, and anger. I sat in there for hours telling them the truth and they still didn't care what I had to say. I kept thinking, *They can't do this! This isn't right!* Then I realized the truth I wasn't just a suspect. I had to be their only suspect.

The detective booked me into the county jail. I remember its distinct smell. It was a mix of stale laundry detergent and inmates who choose to avoid the shower. Jail stunk, literally. As the detective walked me down into a room to get changed, I saw a couple other inmates through the bars across the hallway. They were in orange jumpsuits sitting on their beds, reading their books.

The detective gave me an orange jumpsuit and I was clothed in all the finest jailhouse attire. He walked me over to a tiny, little cell at the end of the hallway and put me in it. All it had was a thin rubber mattress and a combined toilet, sink fixture. I couldn't believe that only twenty-four hours ago it was a wonderful, ordinary morning. Next thing I knew, I was in solitary for a murder that I knew nothing about.

I spent the first couple hours in shock. I was traumatized from the realization that I really had to go through this experience. I struggled to grasp that it was real but at the same time I accepted it, only because I had to. My next line of thinking was, *How am I going to get through this? What should I do now?* My only answer was to be patient and let it run its course. The truth will set you free eventually.

The deputy came up to my cell and asked me if I wanted my phone call. He let me out and walked me to a phone on the wall in the hallway. I did what all young adults would when life turns to chaos, I called home. The call rang a couple times before I heard my mother pick up. She answered and once she heard my voice she started bawling.

"What's going on?" She said as she cried.

"Mom, I don't know, I just went to work and cut my hand. Then the next day, I got arrested for no reason."

"Mayor Cooper's daughter was killed and everyone thinks you did it. We both know rumors spread like wildfire. I know it couldn't have been you. Luke, I remember rocking you to sleep when you were a boy and you don't have it in you to hurt someone, let alone take their life.

Nevertheless, I got you an attorney and he will be there tomorrow to talk to you. We shouldn't talk about the case over the phone so hang in there and remember I love you. Remember what scripture says, 'This too shall pass.' I felt slightly comforted but was still in agony over the situation. I took a long, deep breath.

"Thanks, I love you too and I will see you soon."

The next day, my attorney came to see me. He was a slender man with graying hair and a long pointy nose. I walked in and he stood to shake my hand.

"My name is Mr. Weston. Your mother has hired me to represent you in your case. So, shall we get started?"

He sat down and I followed suit sitting across from him. He told me my case was becoming quite high profile and that usually presents a problem because juries can get pressured to convict. That wasn't the news I wanted to hear. I simply wanted the truth out. I was the wrong guy.

I told him all about the detectives and then about what happened to my hand, as well as what I did that day. He asked if I had witnesses to verify my alibi but I had driven the truck by myself. I told them that my boss saw me at the load site but that was about it.

"I will see what comes across my desk and get back to you."

I asked if I could get out of jail.

"We are working on that too, but for now sit tight and be patient," he said.

Easy for him to say, I thought. He wasn't the one sitting in a concrete room all day long with no one to talk to and nothing to do. He gathered up his paperwork and placed it in his briefcase. Then he said, "I'll get to work." He smiled at me and left. The deputy walked into the attorney's room and escorted me back to my solitary cell.

"Chow!" yelled the deputy as he slid a tray of beans, rice, and a piece of cornbread through a slot in the door. I had been so sick to my stomach I didn't realize that I hadn't eaten lately. The meal was closer to slop than food. I ate about two bites and couldn't handle anymore. I took the small cup they gave us and filled it with water from the sink. *Disgusting!* was the only thought that crossed my mind.

It tasted of rusty metal and a slight trace of dirt. I sat on my bunk and stared at the full tray of garbage and dirty water. It was one thing to sit in a cell by myself but to be hungry multiplied the suffering.

It was quite an experience sitting in a room with little sound and no company. I started to notice the small things. I could hear myself breathing and I counted my breaths. Hours must have gone by doing nothing but that. It was one after another, after another.

I was simply breathing. I noticed how much feeling my skin had. I noticed chills running down my spine from the coolness of the concrete. My senses seemed to be more vibrant to me. Time stood still while I was in there. It felt like I was in a time capsule saving me for the future.

It wasn't all bad because I had plenty of time to think. Also, I never had the ability to reflect on my memories like I could then. It was like watching a movie of my life. I lacked distraction. That was rare in the world.

I also started to forget how bored I really was. It was the only way to cope. If I meditated then the time went by more quickly. I knew the worst thing I could do was focus on being there, so I tried not to. It was a unique experience where my best friend was my mind.

My mind amazed me. The topics that crossed it were so complex. I asked myself about religion. I reanalyzed my priorities in life. I thought more about tragedy than I have ever before. It was amazing to me how people lived their lives thinking that they had it so tough when I would trade them in a heartbeat. I thought of the petty parts of life that used to seem so hard, like not being able to afford a new car. It was like I thought I had problems until I really had problems.

I decided to look at the glass half full though. I picked out several parts of my life that I could thank the Lord for. My parents were alive and I was healthy for the most part. Psychologically, I felt that there was some damage but nothing too catastrophic that wouldn't heal with time.

I hated the waiting. I wanted everything to be cleared up and over instantly. One day in jail was undeserved but it seemed like no one cared. It was a horrible process. It was a waste of valuable time, time I could be using to make priceless memories.

I was in a place where it was almost impossible to stay busy. To get a better understanding of what it is like living in a jail cell, then try sitting in a bathroom for an entire day. Don't do anything besides think. Seconds feel like minutes and minutes feel like hours.

It was early in the morning when a deputy smashed his fist against my solid steel door. "Get ready for court," he said as he walked away. *What's going on now?* I stood up, put on my shoes, and waited by the door. The deputy opened it and escorted me up to the officer station. He put shackles around my ankles and handcuffs on my wrists. He walked beside me up some stairs and through a hall way. I looked at the big brown door that led into the courtroom. I didn't know what to expect. *What was on the other side? What was going to happen?*

The deputy pushed open the door and I proceeded through. I will never forget the look on my mother's face. It wasn't anger or fear. It was a look of complete sympathy. She hurt with me, not for me. That must be what motherly love is. It was a love so pure that she would take a multitude of suffering to save me from slight. I could see that we felt so similar in emotion.

I looked over behind the prosecutor's desk at a lady with pure evil in her eyes. I recognized her face. It was the mayor's wife. She had a look I had never experienced before. It was a dark and wicked look. It was a look of pure hate. She was disgusted at my very existence. I hurt even more at that moment because she didn't know the truth. She had no idea that I literally knew noth-ing about the loss of her daughter. I don't think she really cared though. I think she mourned from the hurt she felt and she needed someone to blame.

I sat down next to my attorney. It took only a couple seconds before the bailiff shouted, "All Rise!" and the judge walked in.

"You may be seated," he said as he walked to his podium.

He sat down and looked directly at me. "I'm Judge Kirkland and I will be presiding in this case. The defendant has been identified as, Mr. Luke Cassidy. He has been charged with murder in the first degree. Do you understand the charges against you, Mr. Cassidy?"

I responded with a lump in my throat.

"I do, Your Honor."

"And, how do you plead?" The judge replied.

My attorney stood immediately and said, "Not guilty, your Honor," before I had a chance to open my mouth. The judge wrote something down on his paper. He looked back at the defense table.

"Our only other subject matter for today is the issue of bond. Mr. Green, you are inclined to speak first," he said.

"Thank you, Your Honor. The prosecution is asking that the defendant has his bond rejected, Your Honor. With his age and lack of maturity, his probability of flight is high. With a charge as serious as this, we are certain he would flee. For the protection of society, we believe that he should be held with no bond until further notice."

The judge shook his head once the prosecutor finished. I didn't like the way it was going. I didn't like the way he looked at me. It felt like he was glaring at me through his small, oval glasses. I felt we didn't have very much similarity and that hurt my case. The judge seemed like he was cut from a different cloth than me. We were simply raised differently and I could tell. He seemed to be a very proud man. He turned back at us and said, "Now, the defense."

My attorney stood and said, "Your Honor, look at this boy. He has the look of innocence on his face. He has many ties to the community and was raised in this town. We are asking for a reasonable bond. As you know the prosecution has the burden of proof and I have yet to be shown what they have to tie my client to the murder. My client's innocence will be proven. We ask for a bond of twenty-thousand dollars. Thank you, Your Honor."

He nodded again after my attorney finished talking. He took a few minutes to think. Everyone in the courtroom sat silently and waited for him to make a decision. I stared at the door leading back to the jail. I dreaded having to go through it again. He finally spoke.

"Well, this case has escalated quickly. There is a lot of emotion when life is lost. It's no surprise that it is exceptionally high when a young lady is the victim. I have to look at society as well as keeping the defendant safe. Therefore, I am going to hold Mr. Cassidy at no bond until further notice to ensure the safety of both parties."

I sighed deeply as he finished. By no means was I excited when they escorted me back into my cell. Part of me was thankful to get the hour out of the room, the other was angry I had to go back in the first place. At least I had something new to think about.

Several hours had past since my first appearance in court. I paced the cell to pass time. I felt so lost, every step I took I felt as if I was walking on air. My sense of reality had dissipated. I felt so alone. It was a horrible nightmare and I kept wondering when I would wake up. Over and over I imagined opening my eyes to see the bland white ceiling of my home but it wasn't coming. I knew it wouldn't but I didn't give up hope that it could happen.

It got so tough I realized I couldn't do it on my own anymore. I did the only thing I felt I could in a time of need. I went back to my Christian roots. The deputy came by and I asked him for a Bible. He brought it to me and I began reading it. It was actually more like talking to it. I had questions, it had answers and for the next several days all I did was read.

The more I read, the more comfortable I became. The Bible told me about the suffering Christ went through. It told me there is a future of hope. It occupied my time and kept my mind focused. I was learning so much about his word. After I finished the entire New Testament, I sat down and prayed. "God, please do not make me go through this alone. Show me you love me and will always be there. Guide me and direct my path. I want your will not mine. I love you so much. In Jesus's name I pray, Amen."

After I prayed, I opened up my Bible and read another scripture that really comforted me. *"I will never leave you, I will never forsake you."* I sat on my bunk and started to think. I asked myself a very important question. *Why?* It wasn't why am I here or why do I deserve this? It was why did this have to happen in order to get me to open the Bible? Why did I only turn to God in times of trouble? Why does everyone seem to only turn in times of trouble? I asked for comfort when times were tough but in my times of satisfaction, I never turned to give God praise.

I felt so selfish, so one-sided. I wanted to think I was the one that made my life good but it was truly all God's blessing. I really didn't do much at all. I paid my bills and made choices to have good things in my life, but God gave me the air to breathe. What could I possibly do without life? What could I accomplish? I could do literally nothing without God.

I felt so irritated with myself. I was disappointed. I wanted to go back in time just to thank God for what he gave me at the good moments. What I didn't realize, even then, was I could still be thanking God. I saw trouble all around me. I looked at my life as if it was ruined. I thought I couldn't thank God because times were so horrible. I thought it was the worst it could get. Why would I thank him in the storm? I had so much to learn, so much room to grow.

Chapter 4

TWO WEEKS WENT BY AND nothing new had happened. The deputy came by and told me that I had court again. *Finally, something is new*, I thought. My days were running together. I thought eventually I would be able to get out and at least have a conversation with someone but they kept me in solitary for my protection. That was what they said anyway. I truly believe they were trying to make me miserable so I would plead guilty. The guards moved me up to the courtroom the same way as before. The courtroom was packed this time around. Reporters were sitting in the back and both sides were full of people.

"All rise!" and everyone stood as the judge came in. It was the same as last time, very formal and on topic. The judge began to speak on the record. "This is the preliminary hearing of State v. Cassidy. The charge is murder in the first degree with Honorable Judge Kirkland residing. Mr. Cassidy, I am here to determine whether or not a crime has been committed and if you have committed it. Keep in mind the burden is not beyond a reasonable doubt, it is more likely than not. Now, shall we get started? Mr. Green, you may call your first witness."

Mr. Green stood and stated, "I call Detective Evans, Your Honor." He walked up to the stand where they swore him in. The prosecutor started asking him questions about his credentials, years in the force and experience. Then he started getting into my case to tie me to the murder.

"Mr. Evans, you questioned Mr. Cassidy, correct?"

"Yes."

"And, in that line of questioning, he admitted to injuring his hand with a blade, correct?"

"Yes, sir, he did."

"And, that weapon was found by the side of the road only a few feet away from the corpse of our victim, correct?"

"Yes."

"It was covered in blood and our victim's cause of death was determined to be from puncture wounds to the chest and neck, correct?"

"Yes, that is correct."

"Your Honor, at this time, I would like to submit into evidence item one and two; the knife received at the crime scene, and a blood type analysis matching our perpetrator and the weapon."

I looked at the picture and it was my knife. After my hand slipped, I dropped it on the ground. I was bleeding and I wasn't thinking about the knife. I would have left it at my feet and took off toward the hospital. I couldn't believe that was how they were tying me to the case. I never saw a body when I stopped but I wasn't looking either. It didn't make any sense to me. People have to know that this isn't right. I put my faith in the judge. He seemed smart and could figure it out and set me free.

The prosecutor finished questioning the detective and called a medical expert to talk about the cause of death. He asked him questions about his credentials too but only did the bare minimum as far as time and cause of death. He finished questioning him and rested his case. The judge turned to my attorney and told us it was our turn. My attorney stood up and to my surprise said, "No witnesses, Your Honor."

I nudged him and asked, "What are you doing?"

He looked back at me. "Just trust me. We will lose the preliminary hearing no matter what we do so we need to wait until trial before we put you on the stand." I shook my head. *Will this ever be over?*

He was right. The judge set trial and gave us plenty of time to prepare. Trial was in almost six months and I didn't have bond. I was stuck in a six-by-nine cell with nothing but my mind and my Bible. I read daylight till dawn, or so I thought. I never knew what time it was because I had no clock. I knew the guards would do their rounds at least every hour so I tried to judge time by that. I also used when I got my meals to tell time. I was fed every six hours, breakfast at six, lunch at noon, and dinner around six at night.

I spent a lot of time in prayer. I wanted to pray like Jesus did though. I never wanted to pray for God to get me out of this or something to that nature. I prayed for His will because I believed that He had a plan for me. I trusted that He saw a future for me that I couldn't see for myself.

I read about the story of Joseph. It was probably one of my favorites because of the way he had to handle adversity. He went to prison for a crime he never committed and I understood what it felt like to be falsely accused. The similarity was what helped me. I also felt it was ironic that his story was in the first book of the Bible because I felt my story of being falsely accused was the beginning of my life story.

I was reading in the book of John when I heard a noise down the hallway. It turned into some yelling and sounded like a scuffle. I heard a couple thumps and a slight scream. I got down on my hands and knees and looked between the crack under the door and the ground. I saw a few guards jogging toward the disturbance. I didn't know what was happening but the noises sounded like a brawl.

I was afraid of jail. I didn't like the feeling of being locked up or the type of people there either. Even though I wasn't around other inmates at the time, I could picture what they were like. The guards were extremely rude. I doubt they started like that but after years of putting up with the worst attitudes in society, I could see how they would become resentful.

One of the hardest parts of solitary confinement was I felt lonely all the time. Being alone became one of my greatest fears.

The thought itself terrified me. I understood what it felt like to an extent but not full blown isolation. I still saw a guard every now and then, but it wasn't as often as I would have liked. In a way, I had to learn to become completely content with myself. It could be all I have one day.

I prayed again that whatever had happened, everyone was safe. I hated violence and I didn't want anyone to be hurt. I looked under the door for any sign of what happened. I waited for several minutes, but no one walked by and nothing happened.

I listened so carefully through my days in county. I tried to listen to peoples' conversations so I could feel like I was a part of them. I missed having camaraderie with people. I felt sensitive physically but even more emotionally. Little things would get to me. I felt like a loose cannon emotionally, not because I wanted to hurt people but because I felt so hurt. I found myself struggling to keep my composure. At times, I would even start to cry for no reason. It was because emotionally, I had so much I wanted to let out but couldn't. I was in no place to be vulnerable. I had to be tough.

Worst of all, I wanted to be selfish. My mentality made me think of myself and what position I was in. It was hard to focus on the positive or see the light in the situation. I only noticed myself, and how tough I had it.

Once I saw the same person get in and out of jail. He was let out and brought back several times during my stay at county. To be blunt, I was jealous. I was never given a chance and I was truly innocent. He was most likely guilty as could be and was let in and out, over and over.

I felt betrayed by the system. It was supposed to fix the problems, not make them. I didn't know that it was the way it was until I went through it personally. It seemed like no one would listen. It made me feel so worthless, like I never mattered to society. It hurt to be disregarded so easily, especially by the town I grew up in. All together it was an awful experience, but at the same time I had the understanding that it can only be as perfect as the people who run it.

The problem is people are very far from perfect. So the flaws we carry as humans will infiltrate our systems. I never should have trusted that it would be any different.

What it came down to was I wanted to know what God had in store for me. I had so many questions. *What kind of future would I have?* I hated the idea that my life was over. I was young and barely started to make an impact on the community. I had always wanted to make the world a better place but that privilege seemed to be slipping from my fingertips. I simply was so beat down that I was losing hope and wouldn't object if my life were to end.

Even at that point, I didn't realize I had a very difficult road ahead of me. I knew I didn't deserve to be on it but I couldn't control my path. I could only walk it or stand still. I had no alternative route. I did have control of one part though, and that was my attitude. I had to look for the silver lining otherwise I would crumble.

I started to question God though. I thought I truly wanted God's will but at the same time I wanted him to fix my problems. I didn't want to suffer any longer. I guess what I am trying to say is I wanted God's will to match my own. But sometimes God doesn't work like that.

Chapter 5

THE NEXT SEVERAL MONTHS DRAGGED on slowly. The only part to look forward to was the meals and they were garbage. I never wanted beans and rice again. I was sick of cornbread, undercooked meals, and unseasoned food. I lost a large amount of body weight because I couldn't stomach the food. I tried to eat it but found myself throwing up because of the tortuous menu. The food I was served was disgusting. It didn't just taste bad, most of the time it was spoiled too. But it was all I had, so I had to eat it.

I found myself getting sick quite often. Some days I was camped right next to the sink. I developed a large distaste for jail. I wanted clean food and a cozy bed to rest in. Even a pillow would have been nice but that was all luxury. I was completely sick of being surrounded by hard, freezing cold, concrete walls. Every day they seemed to close in. I couldn't breathe anymore. It felt like someone was pushing on my chest, it was crushing my diaphragm. I was drowning in nothing but air.

I survived one moment at a time. Deep breaths helped to an extent but I wasn't allowed any fresh air. Even when I took long breaths it still felt like I wasn't getting any oxygen. It was tough and I felt like I was getting closer to suffocating with every second. At moments, simple breathing was all I was capable of.

My mom came to visit as much as they would let her. It was for only fifteen minutes a week. It was in a small room and we were separated by a wall and small glass window. The visit went by nearly instantly. It was the highlight to my week but at the same time it was tough because it was a constant reminder of what I was missing.

I missed her gentle touch and embracing arms. I missed most things about her, even stuff she wouldn't think I would notice. My mom was a very polite, upbeat woman. She had the brightest smile when she laughed and the sound of her laugh was one of a kind. It was more like a quiet yet excited chuckle. Most of the time when she visited, it was hard for her to quit thinking about me being locked up. I am sure it made her depressed but at the same time she was a strong woman.

I just wanted to look into her vibrant brown eyes and tell her everything will work out. I wanted to comfort her at the same time she wanted to protect me. I wanted to go back in time to a simpler time. I wanted to be a kid again and have her hold me. I wanted to know the future and know everything would turn out alright.

The hardest part of visiting was watching her leave. All I wanted to do was sit and talk to her. I wanted to listen to everything she said. I hated the fact that I was missing out on making memories. I really hated jail. It was the first time I had ever hated anything at all.

I couldn't really imagine going through a worse situation. It made me realize how much warfare was fought in the mind. My fight wasn't physical but spiritual. I had to love through the hard times. I had to push through the pain and remain strong. I had to fight hate and not allow it in my life. It may be hard to comprehend but hate is a way of giving the devil a foothold and it will lead to destruction.

I worked through my problems as best I could. I knew the feeling of sickness I felt from watching others be released was wrong. I was jealous of them. In some ways it was justifiable because I was innocent and they usually weren't. But it was still wrong. I struggled because I couldn't imagine being executed for a crime I never committed, but I still woke up to that possibility every day.

I was starting to get really mad at myself for thinking that way. I didn't wish incarceration on anybody. I would rather have everyone be law-abiding citizens. I should have been glad for those people to have another opportunity to change their lives but I found it so easy to point fingers. It was completely wrong to think that way because I knew what it felt like to be at the end of a pointing finger. It really bothered me, so I prayed about it.

Prayer was my go-to play in almost every situation. I wanted to thank the Lord for the positive parts of my life and ask for help with the negative. The truth I needed to realize was with the right perspective there is no such thing as negative. In anything, death or sickness, someway there is always a silver lining. It might not be known at that time, but eventually it will be understood. Sometimes it takes until after death to know the plan God had in store, but that is also the beauty in it. We have to have courage in order to have faith and trusting God isn't always easy. That is why it is majestic, because in the end, when we look back, we can see how perfect and together God's plan always was.

The days were counting down. My trial started the next day and I had a very uncertain future. I continued to pray and thank God for everything I could think of. It made everything easier because I didn't focus on how bad it actually was. I learned there is no such thing as too much prayer and remained constant in it.

My attorney hadn't done a great job keeping in contact with me. I felt like I was left in the dark and my life was literally on the line. He visited me the day before trial to tell me that he was prepared and I had to testify in order to win. I still didn't want to go through with any part of it. The thought of vindication helped my mindset though. I could picture myself at the end of trial. I would be set free and everyone would finally know the truth.

The trial began on a cool, damp morning. It had been raining outside and I could feel the dampness in the air. An odd thought cross my mind, *It's probably raining because the angels are crying. They must know I'm going to get crucified by the town I grew up in.* It was different because I had remained so optimistic before that. The thought of conviction didn't cross my mind. I didn't think a conviction was even possible.

I walked up to the courthouse in shackles just as before. With every step, my muscles seized from fear of the future. I was both excited and terrified. It was time for me to put it all behind but at the same time I didn't want to enter the courtroom.

I walked in and sat down. Everything in the beginning was like the other hearings. The bailiff called the judge in but this time after the judge had spoken the bailiff called in the jury too. They were an average-looking group of people except a few dressed really nice. Some wore their everyday clothes but for the most part, they all wore their nicest apparel.

The one that drew my attention the most was a heavyset man that sat at the end. He was the most noticeable because he had a large stain on the front of his shirt. It looked like he spilled coffee on himself before court. My attorney happened to tell me he was a bus driver. He told me a little about a few of them. One guy was a teacher and another was a military veteran. I always appreciated anyone that served our country.

I stared at the diverse group of people for my first few minutes in the courtroom. There were more women than men. I couldn't figure out if I liked the jury I had or not. They didn't give me any impression on how they saw me. I looked at all of them and they stared back emotionless.

I didn't know what to do, all eyes were on me. If I smiled, they would think I was a sick psychopath. If I cried they would think I was remorseful of the crime. If I showed any emotion it was naturally viewed negatively. I tried to keep my poker face on and show nothing at all but they would probably view that as if I didn't care about what was done. All around it was a losing situation.

The state started with its opening statement. A large picture of Jean was put up right in front of the jury. It was her last school photo taken only weeks before the murder. She was pretty with her white teeth, long blonde hair, and tan skin. The jury melted at the picture of her.

The prosecutor spoke, "Ladies and gentlemen, when you lose a spouse, you become a widow. When you lose a parent, you become an orphan. What are you when you lose a child?" He took a long pause before he spoke again.

"There is no word, because there are no words to explain that kind of loss. I want you to take a good look at this photo." He looked directly at the jury as he pointed his finger at the photo.

"It represents more than what it shows. This picture represents pain, loss, hurt, and so much more."

He then pointed at Jean's parents. Her mother dropped her face into her hands and erupted in tears. I hurt for her too. I didn't understand the type of pain she felt from losing her child. She lifted her face back up and looked at the prosecutor. He turned back at the jury.

"Look into her eyes and try to imagine what it is like having a child stolen from you."

Then he looked at me, or more like glared. He stared sternly into my eyes. I wasn't prepared for that look. That look wasn't something I was familiar with. It was a look of pure, unwavering hate.

"Now, envision the man who stole that child sitting right across from you. Wouldn't you want that man to pay for his actions? Wouldn't you want justice? I want him to pay for stealing a life of a young, beautiful, and ambitious lady. I want justice!"

He continued staring sternly at me as he walked back to his desk. I was afraid to lift my face to look at the jury because of the emotion swirling through the courtroom. I could feel the angry eyes glaring down on me from nearly everyone around. That man was ruthless and the worst part was he was against me.

My attorney stood and shuffled some papers in front of him. He took a minute to let people settle down. I thought it was a wise approach. He walked up to the jury slowly and began his opening statement.

"Ladies and gentlemen, my word for this trial is *imagine*." He turned back toward me and pointed his finger.

"Imagine being in that chair with your life on the line. Imagine people not believing in you. Imagine people despising you for a cold, ruthless murder." He changed his voice to a more sympathetic tone.

"Now, ladies and gentlemen, imagine being innocent. Imagine having nothing to do with the crime committed. Imagine being in Luke Cassidy's shoes. My client is truly innocent. The evidence backs my client's statement for a reason, because it is the truth. It is incumbent that I prove to you why you should believe in him. I believe in him and when jury deliberation starts, I feel confident you will too. Thank you."

He slowly glanced over the jury looking for some validation to his opening. I could see the wheels turning in their minds. It made me feel better but I still didn't feel good about how it was going.

The prosecutor spit poison when he talked. With every word, he made me look guilty. He was very good at his job. He did a good job at making me look like a vile creature, rather than a human being. In my mind I truly thought he didn't believe I was guilty. He would catch himself saying very derogatory words and he held back a couple times. I think it was shocking to him how easy it was to make me look like a monster. His words came out so fluidly and with the possibility I really could be innocent he held back at times.

After the openings, the judge spoke, "Mr. Green, you may call your first witness." He stood up and pulled his suit coat snug against his shoulders. He turned and looked at me when he spoke, "I call Detective Evans, Your Honor."

A few seconds later, Detective Evans entered the courtroom. He walked in with his head held high. His face was emotionless and he walked with confidence. He was dressed in a nice, navy blue suit and a white tie. When he walked by my desk he glared intensely into my eyes. He didn't miss a step as he continued up to the stand. He was sworn in and then casually sat down.

The prosecution started asking him questions. It started with his credentials but quickly moved to the case at hand. His testimony was unclear to me. I knew he was lying. He lied about how I acted during interrogation. He called me arrogant as if I knew I would get away with a ruthless murder. I knew he was lying, and I knew he knew he was lying. Everything he said was a blow to make me look guiltier.

It didn't make sense. Several facts still didn't line up. The blade that punctured the victim was smaller than my knife's blade. *How does the wound get smaller than the size of the blade?* It was physically impossible. I was trying to get my attorney to point it out and pound that into the jury's head. He kept saying, "The jury will pick that up."

They brought up the cut on my hand and told the jury I cut it while a poor, innocent girl was fighting for her life. They said I brutally attacked her. They said I took her life and I showed no remorse. They kept using the words monster or creature, and pounded it into the jury's head. Even I felt like I was less of a human.

Their story didn't make any sense but I couldn't tell if the jury knew it. They seemed to take everything in. They would look at me with a glare and then look back at the detective. I still had no idea what was going through their minds. Some looked like they were confused and sympathetic, but others glared at me as if I was a monster.

Then they said they could put me at the scene of the crime. They found my blood smeared on the oak tree by the side of the road. I could explain that but whether they believed me was a different story. Then they showed a picture of the corpse at the scene. At that point, I had a trickle of sweat run down my temple. I had put it all together and knew the real truth. It was a setup. I would have seen the body if that was where she was when I stopped that day. Someone had to have moved her there after I had left.

I felt so nauseous that I was certain I would vomit. It never occurred but my stomach remained upset for a while. The feeling of disgust was something I hadn't experienced before. It suddenly went away when I saw something I will never forget. I was sitting next to my attorney and looked up at the detective. I saw just a glimpse of what looked like horns coming from the front of his head. They were short and barely poked out the front of his skull.

The weirdest part was they were transparent, but for some reason I was allowed to see them. I don't know how to explain seeing something that was clear. Basically, I could see them and see right through them at the same time. It was the glare and outline that was most visible.

My knees began to shake and I started to sweat profusely. Next thing I knew his face started to change too. It looked like his flesh was starting to melt off his face. It started to droop down off his forehead and his eye sockets. It was like all his humanity and honor was slipping from his body to be replaced by revulsion and carnage. I couldn't stand to look at him anymore. It hurt my soul to glimpse at something so wrong. I turned my head and looked at my attorney. He never noticed a thing. I looked back and in a blink everything seemed normal again. It was the most terrifying experience of my entire life.

I felt a blanket of fear come over me. It was so powerful I started to shake, and then the tears started to rush from my body. I was scared and lost. I didn't know what had happened or how to react to it. Then instantly, that extreme low was replaced by an immeasurable high. I was uplifted by something of pure grace. It was like something was trying to tell me it is going to be *okay*. I had a sudden calmness come over me that felt tranquil. I wasn't worried, even in the slightest. My life on earth seemed irrelevant. I still cared about what was going on, but at the same time it didn't matter what happened because I knew my life was part of a perfect plan.

I had never experienced such a simple serenity. My thoughts seemed clearer and my vision felt sharp. It was like I was in a different atmosphere than everyone else. I could still see everything around me and knew where I was at, but it felt like for the first time in my life the messaged was received.

I felt a soft hand graze down my cheek to my shoulder and gentle lips brush against my ear. I felt it start to whisper in my ear. I was comforted and felt at bliss. I was so curious to what it was. I turned suddenly to see it.

In an instant, everything snapped back to normal. I was breathing heavily and my head was pounding. I looked around and nobody seemed to have seen anything. The trial was going on the same as

I remembered. Everyone was listening to the testimony but me. I didn't care anymore. I think I was in shock.

No words can explain my feeling of peacefulness from whatever tranquility that was. When I saw whatever was happing to the detectives face, I felt terrified. After the peace, I didn't know what to feel. It was a hurricane of fear, anxiety, peace, and hope.

That detective had evil in his heart and I could see it, or at least it was exposed to me. The prosecutor seemed just as putrid. When I looked at the jury, my heart sank. I could see into them as well. They believed the lies. They thought I was a monster. It didn't matter what my attorney did, the jury had fell victim to those demons. They were deceived and blinded from the truth.

"All rise for the reading of the verdict," the judge stated.

The jury spokesman stood in his black suit. He looked at me and spoke with no words of sympathy. "The jury finds the defendant Luke J. Cassidy, guilty of murder in the first degree."

I didn't speak. I didn't think. All I did was sit there with a wave of terror running over me. It wasn't just any fear, it was a distinct fear. It was the fear of the unknown. I had fear of what was going to happen to me, fear of my future. I heard weeping behind me but didn't have but a sliver of time to glimpse at my family who still backed me in those stands. Tears flowed down their faces as if it was the end and I was gone forever.

I didn't have the courage to look over at the prosecution. I could only imagine what they looked like though. I couldn't comprehend someone experiencing joy at the destruction of someone else's life. But I was certain it had happened. It showed how true the Bible is. We can be of a very selfish nature. Only humans can justify destroying another to feel better about oneself.

The bailiff brought me out of the courtroom almost immediately after the conviction. My attorney's face was in disbelief when he heard the verdict. With the lack of evidence, he believed they couldn't convict me. They had no proof to say I committed the murder. The case was built on hearsay, it wasn't undisputable facts. He knew that and I knew that, but at that point it didn't matter.

He took a second to look me in the eye before the officer booked me back into jail. He didn't have much to say besides, "This is going to be a long road." It wasn't his fault I was convicted, he didn't know what he was up against. If it had only been people in the courtroom I would have walked free. He left me with a look of shock, hurt, and deep sadness on his face. He knew an innocent man was going to spend the rest of his life in prison.

Chapter 6

I WILL ALWAYS REMEMBER THAT first day pulling up to the prison. The rolls of silver, shining, razor wire glistened in the sun. I would almost call the sight beautiful. It was better than plain concrete anyway. The razor wire drew my attention the most. They hovered over the top of the massive concrete walls. The only structure higher than the walls was the enormous towers at every corner of the prison. Entering the prison felt foolish. It was like stepping into a trap on purpose, but also not having a choice.

The bus driver pressed on the gas as a black cloud of smoke erupted out of the tailpipe. The bus moved slowly through the gate. Guards were surrounding the bus checking under it for any sign of contraband. I stared at everything new outside the bus. It was hard to get a clear view through the barred windows but I was still mesmerized by the sight of the prison.

We had apples and a sandwich that day for lunch. I wasn't a huge fan of apples so I gave it to the man sitting next to me on the bus. He was older than me but not by too much. He had long, red hair that flowed down past his ears. I handed him the red apple and he gave me a nod.

"Thanks man, I could sure use the extra food," he said. I gave him a nod and he reached out his hand to shake mine.

"I'm Jesse James Harper, but some call me Outlaw. I still prefer Jesse but I'll respond to either. What about you? What do you call yourself?"

I struggled to open my mouth. I hadn't talked to anyone for quite a while.

"I hope you didn't forget," he said as I stuttered, "I'm—I'm Luke."

He looked at me with a crooked smile on his face, "And he speaks," he said sarcastically. He looked out the window, through the bars on the bus.

"I'm not excited for this," he said as he shook his head in disbelief.

"Me neither," I responded.

"So, how much time did the man get you for?"

I didn't know how to respond. *What if he judged me?* I decided instantly honesty was my best option.

"I got life, without the possibility of parole," I replied.

He shifted his head back slightly as I told him and his eyes lit up. He was obviously shocked at my response.

"Wow, the long haul," he said.

He smirked at me and said something that made more sense at that moment than anything throughout the entire ordeal.

"It could be worse."

I didn't like to think about that. Getting life in prison for a crime I didn't commit seemed like it was the worst that could happen. But at least I still had my health and my family. I didn't feel it was greedy to want my freedom as well, but I still had something to be thankful for. I simply missed a lot of aspects of life. I wanted to be able to roam around and enjoy nature. I wanted to be able to choose what I did on a daily basis. I wanted to make memories with those that I loved.

Throughout my entire life, I never realized that the ability to do simple tasks was a luxury, not a burden. I would be excited to wash my car or take out the trash. Most of all, I wanted to be happy again. I hadn't had any fun through my long months in county. I wanted to laugh and smile. I wanted to take back all those moments I had taken for granted.

I talked to Jesse for awhile. He told me about him wanting to be like the cowboy Jesse James, so he robbed a bank. He made a joke out of it. We talked about how he should have robbed a train if he wanted the full experience. Anyway, the way he told the story was hilarious. He didn't hurt anyone and his decision to pull the heist was so impromptu it made me laugh. The heist still didn't turn out like he expected. He got fifteen years for it and never made it into the vault.

He sarcastically said he did it for the life experience and he never wanted the money, but I suspected that was a lie. He was an upbeat person and seemed happy even though he was in prison. He actually seemed normal, as normal as a stranger would be expected to act anyway. It was official. I had made my first friend in prison.

I didn't know if I should call him a friend though. I questioned how trusting I should be in the prison system. He seemed like a decent guy but I barely knew him. I had so many questions for myself. *What am I going to do here?*

We all stood up to leave the bus. One by one, we shuffled down the aisle and took those few steps to the ground. I distinctly remember the shock that rushed through my leg as I stepped onto prison ground. It was like stepping onto a battlefield. I felt my knees buckle as I realized what I had just done. I was finally there. *Welcome to the Yard,* I thought. That was slang for what everyone called the prison.

My behavior was completely different than the other men getting off the bus. They definitely intimidated me. They had a certain strut as they stepped off. Chest out, chin up was the way they walked. Almost every man stepping off the bus knew how to act in a prison environment. I stood out in the area, probably because I was the only one that wasn't prepared to fight.

Most looked the part too. They had shaved heads and tattoos all over their bodies. Some even had them on the front of their face. Some of the tattoos were actually creative but most I didn't like. I saw one man with his wife's name on his neck, another had horns on his forehead and skulls down his forearm. The craziest tattoos to me were the ones with human nudity on the back of their heads or arms. I couldn't comprehend why people would want to put something like that on their body.

One of the hardest experiences to explain is the constant glares guys gave each other. They looked at me like they wanted to kill me. I didn't know what I did or why they might feel that way, but the looks were very dark. It wasn't just the looks either. It was the all-around hate that some had for each other.

My best guess was that it was an initial defense mechanism. People had to live with their back against the wall until they had brothers to watch their back for them. It wasn't wise to be quick to trust in prison. Otherwise, it could turn out bad. People turned on each other all the time and for many reasons. It was like a jungle— survival of the fittest.

I did the only thing that had worked for me in times of trouble. I prayed, "Lord, please protect me. I'm so scared of this place and I don't want to live in fear. I want to live for you. Please help me stay focused. I know it's in your will for me to be here but please comfort and watch over me. In Jesus's name I pray, Amen."

The looks didn't stop but I decided I couldn't change that. Prison wasn't my type of atmosphere. It was surreal to me that I was there. For a while, I felt that I was walking around in a dream, like everything I saw was in a dreamlike state. Initially, I didn't know how to survive but I learned quickly.

I had only been in prison for a couple hours and I already felt as if people wanted to hurt, use, or even kill me. I couldn't comprehend a life in there. It was different from county or any other experience I had ever endured. At least in county, I was alone and didn't have the threat of someone trying to hurt me.

I looked up at the wall and saw a sign stating, "Inmate Intake." I looked down in shame. Never in my life did I imagine myself entering a maximum security institution, especially this one. It was built for the most violent killers and predators. Being in a maximum security prison was different because the level of violence. Most people there had a life sentence or close to, so they really couldn't get any more time.

Then there was me, a young Christian kid that hadn't hurt anyone in my entire life. The worst part was in the system, I was in the same category as real killers, but I had never committed murder. I didn't know how to kill, even to protect myself, and yet I was surrounded by experienced killers. It wasn't a good situation to be in.

When I walked into my cell for the first time, I didn't realize that I was about to meet a very special person. The man I was about to meet would become one of my greatest friends and influence me for the rest of my life.

I finally made it to my cell. I was exhausted from the traveling and constant awareness of my surroundings. I wanted to rest but the adrenaline kept me going. I stepped in the cell and to my surprise, a very pleasant man was sitting up on the top bunk with his feet dangling over. He looked nothing like the rest of the population. He didn't have any tattoos and had bright, white teeth. I wasn't scared of him. I instantly felt the most comfortable I had all day.

He hopped down instantly as I walked in. He was polite and took initiative to introduce himself first. He reached out to shake my hand.

"Hi, I'm Gabriel but I go by Gabe. What's your name?" I hesitantly shook his hand even though he seemed nice. I was still in a little shock over the day's activities. I tried to act normal.

"Luke," I replied politely.

I was shy and hesitant to trust, or even talk to anyone. For all I knew, he could be a serial killer. It was like being in a horror movie but it was actually real life. I found myself starting to struggle to breathe again. I gasped for air and felt my anxiety peak. I knew I was about to have a panic attack. I felt myself starting to hyperventilate. It felt like trying to breathe through a straw and the walls started closing in.

Gabe looked at me and calmly said, "Breathe." My face must have been turning red from my panic attack. He stared into my eyes and told me to take deep breaths like he was. I followed suit and we were both taking deep breaths until I started to calm down.

He was so much different than the rest of the men I had encountered. The look on his face had compassion. He cared about my well-being and I was still a stranger to him. That may not be such a big deal on the streets but in prison, that was huge. He made me feel that prison could be different than what I had experienced or maybe just one man was different than the rest. Sometimes in life, one man is all it takes to change everything.

"You okay?" he asked in a clear, compassionate voice.

I was still struggling to catch my breath. After I started to calm down, I walked over to the concrete wall and knocked on it a couple times. That was the only way I could decide if I was in a nightmare or not. If it hurt, then I knew I wasn't dreaming. I knew I was finally in prison and it was real. I wasn't going to wake up for trial and everything would work out. I was really there and I could do absolutely nothing to change it. I hated how the system had played out.

I turned back to Gabe and nodded my head to signal I was fine. He knew I wasn't but didn't pressure me with any questions. Gabe was a little strange to me. He looked like a guy that would have everything going for him, but he was locked in prison. I wanted to know why but I didn't want to ask either. I didn't want the reputation of being nosy.

Gabe was taller than me and he had good features. His chin looked strong and cut, but his smile was his most welcoming feature. Men in prison and even on the streets usually didn't have such a loving glow when they smiled. It was a smile that seemed like he had been through a lifetime of experiences. He was young though. Not as young as me, but he looked like he was in his mid-twenties. He had a clean cut look. Nice blonde hair and finely groomed stubble on his face. It amazed me that someone could keep themselves looking like they just stepped out of a magazine with what little we had in there. For the most part, he was what women would call a handsome, young man.

Also, I found that he was easy to talk to. I was shy and tried to keep quiet, but he seemed like he didn't judge me. It was like he actually cared and had a genuine gentle spirit. That first night after I warmed up a little bit, we sat and talked about every subject we could think of. We had a lot of similar opinions on our topics. We talked politics and religion. We talked about corruption of society and how greed and lust are some of man's biggest downfalls.

Gabe was really intelligent. He spoke very carefully and packed his words full of wisdom. I had spent very little time with him and yet it felt as if we had been friends our entire lives. I simply knew we would develop a brotherly love for each other.

It was different from all the time I spent by myself in county. I enjoyed having the company of a cellmate. I loved having the ability to have a discussion. I could get feedback or advice. It was a blessing that I had overlooked at times in my life. I had studied scripture for months and in that time I didn't get the luxury of another's opinion on God's word. It brought me an entirely new perspective.

When we spoke of scripture, Gabe was also well-educated. We grew together because of our different perspectives. He saw some parts of scripture through one lens and me through another. I loved the way we grew together with our discussions. In the Bible, it is called fellowship. We made each other better because we were both equally yoked and similar in our walk with God. It was a unique type of relationship where we mentored each other.

I loved the security I had with Gabe but that type of relationship was extremely rare. With everyone else, it wasn't like that. I was young and they noticed that, so they tried to extort me with fear. I didn't want any part of it and stayed out of their view, so they didn't pursue it much after that. I think at times they forgot I was even there.

Inmates are a different breed of people. They adapt to their environment and most tend to learn how to be very observant. They become very good at watching and learning the minor habits of people. Then they take advantage and manipulate to get an advantage.

I have seen inmates notice something small, like a wedding ring on a guard, and use it to develop a friendship. Then eventually, they would gather enough trust to get the guard to smuggle in contraband. Usually it starts with something small and harmless, but escalates into something as serious as weapons or drugs.

Over the first few days, I learned the layout of the prison. The prison itself was shaped in a giant square. Outside there was a massive concrete wall that surrounded the perimeter. It had giant towers on every corner. The walls were several feet over my head and had razor wire so big it felt like it stared me in my face.

I had a lot of questions about the prison, so I searched for the information before I found out first hand. I learned about the different blocks and how they classified the inmates in them. The blocks started at A and went through K.

A-block was processing and mainly a guard only facility. That was where new inmates entered and guards had a break room there too. B-block was also known as The Hole. I knew if I ever got in trouble while in prison, that would be my punishment. I didn't know much else besides it was a completely locked down area. That meant inmates were cuffed and escorted everywhere they went.

C-block was basically the insane asylum. If a person couldn't cope in general population, they would be sent there. Basically, it was for the mentally ill. It had suicide prevention rooms and full-time healthcare. There were a few places that weren't known as blocks, like laundry, kitchen, and the chapel. They were located in between the units in different locations.

D through K-block was inmate housing. There were many differences to how we were housed though. It was based on violence and crime, also by race. The more serious the system saw the criminal, the higher up he would go in housing. K-block was for the most violent inmates. It was also all gang members. It was a credential in order to be housed there. Death and fighting were second nature to those men.

I was in J-block, along with several hundred other inmates. It was only slightly less violent than K-block. We were separated from

K-block by a room called the bubble and a metal door. The bubble was basically a glass square where the guards controlled the doors and watched the inmates.

The prison as a whole was massive. The tiers were enormous with cell doors spanning from every wall a few stories up. The middle of the tier had metal tables and chairs bolted to the ground. Some inmates played cards, others used the tables to draw or simply sit and talk.

I found the most unique part of every tier was it was like its own society. People came from different cultures and backgrounds. They had different tendencies and reacted to problems differently. The prison population had a culture of its own and it was all new to me.

I didn't see a lot of people from other tiers. The guards tried to keep rival gangs and races away from each other to keep down the violence. We still intermixed at times, like chow or church, but mostly during yard time.

Yard time was when we went outside. Most inmates were outside a majority of their time because that was where everything happened. If I ever needed anything, yard time was where I could find it. It was basically like the market out on the streets. That was where the ball field was located. The ball field was a plain grass field with nothing to it. It had a weight pile and was surrounded by a dirt path that some inmates would jog on. But other than that, it didn't have much.

Chapter 7

MY MOST DOMINANT EMOTION IN the first few days of prison was fear. I was constantly looking around watching my surroundings because that was what others did. I thought of prison as if it was the jungle. It had a hierarchy like the jungle. The apex predators controlled the behavior of the other animals, like if a lion went to the watering hole the zebras would scatter. It was the same in prison; inmates would avoid those that could hurt them.

I remember the first fight I saw. It escalated so quickly because everyone there seemed to have a short fuse. There were two men standing together having a conversation. One man was taller with a thin, long build and the other was bald with a compact muscular build.

The taller man was standing with a hot cup of coffee in his hand. They looked like everyone else having a casual conversation. They started feuding with each other over something. I was too far away to hear what they were talking about but it quickly escalated into yelling. Within seconds, the tall man splashed his smoldering hot coffee into the other's face. The guy grasped his face immediately and began to scream as he dropped to his knee. I will always remember how distinct and awful the sound of his scream was.

I figured that was the end of the fight but it was only the beginning. He was defenseless but the tall man didn't care. He sent a fury of fists into his head. The smaller man fell from his knee to the ground and that wasn't the end of the fight either. He mounted him and continued punching the man. Fist after fist exploded into his body. The fight started with screaming but it didn't take long before he couldn't muster up the air to scream.

By the time the guards stopped the fight, blood covered both the ground and his disfigured face. Blood spurted out from a large gash in his lip and his eyes were swollen shut. The rest of his face was red and slightly blistered from the burn. He had become unconscious before the majority of the beating was over. I felt so sorry for him. I couldn't do anything to help him. I was scared and I froze because I had never seen a fight like that before. We were locked down before I saw what happened to him after that.

Lockdowns happened when violent events took place, so they were often. We were escorted to our cells and not let out until the warden cleared us. The worst part about the fight was how the rest of the inmate population reacted. Nobody else cared about him. His unconsciousness didn't stop the brutality of the attack. If anything, it made it easier.

He didn't hold back either. He hit him as hard as he could with every swing. In a normal society, men could tell when the other had enough. I imagined anyway because I never had been in a fist fight. In prison, it was different. That barrier didn't exist. Inmates could continue reading a book or holding a conversation while someone else was getting beat into a coma. It was disgusting to me.

To the guards, it was only a job. They wanted to do the bare minimum and an inmate's death was collateral damage. They worried about their own safety first so if they were in danger, then they wouldn't even try to help. They reacted slowly too. They were in no hurry to put themselves in harm's way. It was a lot safer to remove a motionless body than to stop a brutal attack. I figured that prison would be horrible but I never imagined it would be the way it was. I thought there would be fights but not ruthless attacks on men until they were in a coma or dead. I was scared, very scared.

I struggled to cope in the environment I was in. It was nice having Gabe around, so at least someone could help in the hard times. I was still mostly alone. I wasn't the type of recruit gangs looked for because I was young and unintimidating. In fact, I was probably one of the nicest guys in the entire prison. Overall, I was thankful that I had at least one friend. I loved the chemistry and similar thoughts we shared. Even on the oddest of subjects there was some type of similarity.

We were cellmates so naturally, we looked out for each other. It was a smart idea to group together and watch each other's back, so we headed almost everywhere together. We were together for chow, the library, and recreation. I liked it though. He was my best friend and everyday our friendship only grew.

I started to grow curious about him. I couldn't figure out why such a good man would be in prison. I wanted to ask but at the same time I couldn't. Most were there for being very violent or because they were a menace to society. I had a different feeling about Gabe. My theory was he was in the wrong spot at the wrong time, but it was only a theory. His attitude about prison was different. He almost acted as if it was an honor to be there. He must have known something that I didn't because he had a bigger picture in mind.

I decided to ask him a few questions about his experience with prison. The first question I asked him was, "How long are you going to be here?"

He responded vaguely, "As long as it takes."

I didn't know what it meant but I felt he was trying to avoid the question so I backed off a little. That question was almost a trick question because most can tell the seriousness of the crime by the length of their sentence.

My question changed into, "Well, how long have you been here?"

He responded with, "In the scheme of things, not too long."

I was completely confused. By that point, I knew he didn't want to lie to me or tell me the truth. I figured that my best option would be to never ask again, so I didn't. I respected him enough to give him his privacy. For all I knew, he could have been there for years already and have lifetimes to go. Regardless, it was his business, not mine.

Time was different in prison. It moved at a different pace. Most people naturally assume that time moves slower but in some ways it doesn't. I found that my days went by too fast to remember. It was because of the lack of new memories. When I was free, I could make a lot of different memories in a week, so in retrospect time seemed slower, but in prison the days were the same, so I would forget how much time went by. It was hard to recall any certain timetables for events because my days moved as one giant blob.

Gabe made me feel so comfortable but he was mysterious at the same time. Even the small things about him were different than others. People still laughed in prison but when Gabe smiled, I could see the joy in his heart. I wanted that same contentment and view on life. I didn't know much about his life but I knew that he had a great outlook. Let's face it, we were both at the bottom of the barrel, but Gabe was happy even in that situation.

It made me think of biblical people. I remember reading about Paul in the Bible. He said something about being content with much and with little. I could see a similarity with Gabe. We both had nothing and yet he was blissful every time I saw him. It did a lot for me. It inspired me to be happy no matter what I was going through. It was easier said than done though. Life in prison was up and down, but if I looked forward to something, it seemed to help pass the time.

I started by looking forward to the meals. They were still garbage but it was different than the food in county. Then after I got bored with that, I looked forward to daily activities. I exercised, prayed, and developed a daily routine which all helped a ton. I looked forward to growing in my relationship with God and with my friend.

I started to notice the small things too. I studied Gabe by what he said and how he acted when he didn't know I was watching. I was searching for whatever it was that made him such an enjoyable person in an awful environment. I came to the conclusion that Gabe was a man full of love. He had a sincere, pure love for people. He wasn't going through the motions for a label of being a good person. He showed me that love was a way of life, not just a type of feeling. He was totally content with others being more important than he was.

That was a hard type of mentality to have, especially in prison. People were vultures there. They would take everything from him, even what he needed to survive. He never gave more than he could afford but he was also generous with his time and advice. For everyone else, it was survival mode while being incarcerated. They were both hoarders and scavengers, and if I had something someone else wanted, they would try to take it.

It was hard to adapt to at first. The first couple months were all about adaptation. The new environment was cruel and I had to learn to get loud. I had to choose to eat or be eaten, kill or be killed. I began to change with the environment. It was a transformation of my mind that was more negative than anything, but I had to learn to survive. My fuse had shortened and I was more accepting of violence and conflict. I never embraced it but it was a part of my life and I had to deal with it. Fights were common, gangs ran the place, and I learned that some men lust over other men. I had to accept that was what my life was going to be.

When I first walked into prison, I learned about the term prospecting. It was basically the same as recruiting, except it was for gangs. They had to keep numbers up to remain in power. Gang members would look for the "new fish" entering prison and decide if they wanted them to be part of their gang. I had no intention of being part of something like that. Control of my life was for God, not a man. That mindset cost me a lot at first. I don't want to get too graphic but it was torturous.

I was jumped, beaten, and crushed all because I refused that lifestyle. It ranged from simple vocal abuse to new prospects attacking me to earn their keep. It was hard and depression would have been part of my life if it wasn't for God. The sins happening to me were not the worst of it. What really hurt was seeing others indulge in sin and not feel remorse.

I hated to see another human being blinded from the truth. They were lied to and told it was "okay." It was the promotion of hate and I hated that. It was simply the blind leading the blind. The problem was where they were leading them to. It was tough on me having men sin against me but what hurt the most was when they sinned against their own body. I saw man as art, crafted by the hand of God; and when I saw that get corrupted, I really struggled to keep my mouth shut.

I was walking back to my cell when I saw a glimpse of a man lying with another man in their cell. My stomach churned and it made me feel sick. I hated prison and I had only endured it for a slim moment compared to most. I was disgusted that men were bound by that.

Prison was so overcome with sin that the people didn't even realize how dark it was. They couldn't see what I saw because they were so callus in their own ways. It was normal to them. They didn't use the words morality, integrity, or honesty. It wasn't in their vocabulary. I was raised in a Christian home. At least I had a little bit of a Christian foundation but these men had none.

I felt sorry for them. They didn't know the Lord or had turned their back on Him. Either way, I still felt hurt to see what I saw. I was flustered with emotion because I had never seen two men together. I would have rather never noticed and didn't intend to see it but I did. I didn't know what to do or think. I asked myself several questions like, *Is it really my business what others do? Should I turn the other cheek? Should I condone that type of behavior?* It is clear in the Bible that God made one man and one woman for each other.

I ran into my cell with sweat trickling down my temple and across my forehead. I was still appalled at the sight of homosexuality. I kept thinking back to the Bible. It unmistakably states a man and a woman are to become one flesh before God. I had sadness and hurt crossing my heart, but when I spoke, anger came out. I yelled at Gabe as he was sitting on his bunk reading his book.

"I don't understand this place!" He turned to me and smiled. It was like he knew what I saw before I even told him what had happened.

"It's because you still have hope."

My face turned red when I told him what I had seen. He listened to everything I had to say before he decided to speak. I told him everything I was feeling. I asked him questions like, "Should I say something or try to help? What should I do?" I was frantic as I talked to him and he calmly replied to me.

"Some people choose to betray biblical principles for their own desires. They are immoral and the fate that awaits them…" He paused for several seconds. He looked up as he reflected on his memories. A tear strolled down his cheek and I realized how devastated he actually was. He was hurting with me and I felt the emotional connection between us. I knew at that point he was my Christian brother. He calmly regained himself and started to speak again.

"Luke, you need to understand what you're looking at and really focus. Read the subtext of the situations rather than what is blatantly obvious. The people that are choosing their lusts are only trying to fill a void inside themselves. They turn to the flesh when it's the spirit that's thirsting for satisfaction. The spirit thirsts for one thing and that's a relationship with God. The people that have turned their back on God are obvious. Just look around, most men in here already have, and some will never turn back."

He was so calm and subtle as he spoke but the topic was serious. He was the only one I felt comfortable talking to and I trusted him. I was afraid of talking to anyone else on the yard because they may be bound by the sin I was trying to avoid. I realized how fast I had to learn discretion.

"Luke, you still have a lot to learn. I have seen evil for a lot longer than you have but that doesn't mean I can change it. It's as much a part of earth as good is. That's what free will is all about. Having the right to choose what path you will take.

You know that feeling when you do something good or the horrible feeling you get when you do something wrong. You decipher that feeling from the same source. God's law is written in everyone, even if they don't know it or don't believe it. It doesn't matter, it's still there. Some people call it your conscience but they don't truly understand what it is. Some people have allowed Satan to get a foothold in their lives so they are less sensitive to it. But it's still there regardless of whether or not it is felt. It simply gets magnified the closer you get to God.

That's why you would feel guilty if you were to steal. He holds His people more accountable because they know better. Sin is still going to be in your life but the fight against it is what matters. Don't let it overtake you because the moment you think you have it beat is when it strikes the hardest. Remember to always be wary and guard your heart."

It made a lot of sense what Gabe was saying to me. He seemed to always have in-depth responses to my questions. He cared about the answers and didn't want to steer me wrong. He acted as if he had been through all these questions himself. It was nice to have a friend who understood my future was his past. To me it validated scripture even more, *"Nothing is new under the sun."*

I slowly sat down on my bunk and picked up my Bible. Gabe was resting up on his bunk as well. I looked around the cell as I was thinking. It was so compact and bland. All we had was a metal desk that was fused to the concrete wall and a combined toilet-sink fixture. That was about as luxurious as my furniture was going to get. I knew at that moment that was the most I would ever have. It didn't matter how hard I worked or what I did that was my life.

I was alright with it though. I learned really quickly that I had to use my life for more than momentary gain. I could use it to help people and seek my validation in the promotion of those around me. The truth was, I could really live without the distraction of everyday life. I could accomplish a lot that some others would never have the opportunity to do.

My thoughts changed back to my conversation with Gabe. I was deeply hurting from what I saw in the world. It was hard to focus on the world and never notice how much evil irradiated from it. It was a place where people stole, lied, and killed. It was an evil place and it bothered me that I couldn't change it. But my views changed quickly. It was also a place of beauty. It was a place where people loved, honored, and respected each other. For a second, I thought I might have seen the world through God's eyes. He had to see the good in the world and so should I.

I laid down on my bunk as I continued to think. The hard mat I was given for a mattress was not much better than concrete. I shuffled my body to get in a more comfortable position. It helped a little. I couldn't help but get irritated that I was there. I felt my life had been ruined. I asked myself, *Why is God exposing me to this place?*

I felt it was time to speak.

In my head, I just simply talked, "God, please, comfort me. I need you to help me, to surround me, and watch over me. I can't do this by myself. I know I'm not strong enough. Don't leave me." The tone in my head changed to a more thankful voice.

"Also, thank you for the blessings I do have. I haven't forgotten everything you do for me. I needed a friend like Gabe to help comfort me. He is right. I need to guard my heart and I can only do that with your help. Thank you for Gabe, he is a good friend and has helped me more than he knows. God be with me and my loved ones. Thank you, in Jesus's name I pray, Amen."

Chapter 8

"HEY SON, IT IS GOOD to hear your voice. How are you holding up in there?" My mother asked.

It was good to talk to her. For the time being, I could only talk to her on the phone because she lived on the other side of the state. I missed my parents. After the conviction, it became very hard to communicate. I called about twice a month and wrote them letters, but that was nothing like actually seeing them.

I missed the way they looked at me. I had always been their pride and joy. I missed even the most irrelevant parts about them, like the way my mom's nose would scrunch when she laughed really hard. I missed parts about my dad too, like when he was really proud of me he would struggle to hold back the tears. I will never forget the way his eyes would glass up.

I missed the simple parts too. We would almost always eat dinner together. It meant the world to me having such a close family but once I graduated high school, I was driven to make a name for myself. I came from a lower class family. Most months we barely managed to squeeze by. I wanted a different life for my children and I was prepared to earn it. It all changed when that opportunity was stolen from me though.

My thoughts drifted back to my conversation with my mom.

"I'm doing as well as I can. I really want to see you. It's hard only talking on the phone. I have so much to tell you. When are you going to come visit me?"

She sounded hurt when she spoke to me. Her voice cracked and quivered with every word, and at times she struggled to speak at all. It was like she was talking to a ghost, like her son had been killed, but we could still communicate. It hurt me too. I wanted a normal life with her but it didn't work out that way. I knew she didn't see me as a failure for ending up in prison but I wondered if she thought she was. She wasn't there to protect me and I think she blamed herself. I knew it was in no way her fault but she simply loved me too much to watch me hurt.

At that point in my life, I didn't quite understand the love for a child. I related it to how the Lord loves me but those two loves still differed. I doubt man can love in the same caliber as God because his love is so perfect and endless. But I do believe that the love for a child is the closest type of love we can experience to God's love.

I started to reminisce about the memories I had of my mother. In fact, my earliest childhood memory was with me and my mother. I must have been about two or three years old but I still had the clarity of what happened in my mind.

It was a simple memory. It wasn't anything extravagant like a family vacation or wedding. It was me simply walking up to my mother as she prepared lunch for my father. I looked outside the screen door to see dad approaching the house from a distance. I turned back to my mom and gestured I wanted food too.

She knew me better than anyone in the world. She loved me so much more than herself. We couldn't even measure the comparison. It was a symbol for me, that the littlest details in life can sometimes make the grandest impact.

My parents' love for me reminded me of a story I had once heard. It was about a father who had two children. He loved them so much that it didn't matter to him how they messed up, he still forgave them. He still disciplined his children though, so they would learn to live properly.

One day both his children screwed up very badly. He was put in a situation where he had to choose what son should be put to death and what one should live. They were both great children but still sinners. He wept and fell to his knees refusing to allow his children he loved so much to be put to death.

"Take me, take me instead!" He yelled bawling.

At that point, the father had an understanding of what Jesus did and why he died for us. Someone had to pay the debt for our sins and Jesus did that because he loved us. It is astonishing how powerful that love is.

My mind went back to my conversation with my mother.

"Your father and I are going to make arrangements to come see you next weekend. We will find a hotel and stay there for the night. We have been trying to come since the conviction but we couldn't afford to go yet. We are going to borrow some money from the church to get there though. Dad has been working over time because we want to make it up there so badly but money has been very tight."

"It's okay. I know you have been trying. I'm glad you can come soon. I can't wait to see you. I love you." I could tell she was crying on the other end of the phone.

"I love you too," she said in a soft, sad voice.

The next few days were typical. I wanted to talk to mom on the phone but I didn't have access to use it. We lived a simple life with simple means. All our money went into trying to keep me from prison. If I would have known I was going to go to prison anyway, I would have represented myself to save the cash.

I wanted to see them so badly. I missed them so much. I didn't want anything to affect me getting to see my parents. I did everything I could to avoid the violence and the corruption. I couldn't stress how excited I was for mom and dad to come see me. I knew it had been just as hard on them as it had been on me. They lost their only son, even though I was still living. I couldn't wait for them to visit me for the first time. I hadn't seen them since my stay in county jail.

It was the day before they said they were going to come see me. Excitement was an understatement. The thought of joking and laughing with my parents would make my year. They were all I had.

The entire day all I could think of was, *I will see them tomorrow, I will see them tomorrow.*

That night a prison guard showed up at my cell door. He pulled me from my cell and told me he needed to talk to me. I didn't think much of it because it was common to be pulled from my cell. Gabe stayed on his bunk and paid little attention to what was going on. I knew something was up when I saw the look on the guard's face. He looked very serious and sympathetic. As I stepped out, he looked down slightly.

"I don't really know how to say this but I just got word that your parents were in a car accident."

It took me completely by surprise. I didn't say anything. I knew he was wrong. They couldn't have had the right guy. My dad had never been in a wreck his entire life. He was the most cautious driver I knew. Regardless, if it was true, I worried if they were alright.

"Are they okay? Did they have to go to the hospital?"

Then I saw another look I had never experienced before. The way his eyes watered and the slight frown as he spoke. It was the first time a guard showed any compassion. He was affectionate toward me. It was rare to get any emotion from anyone on the yard because it was a sign of vulnerability, even to the guards.

I don't think the guard cared what people thought of him at that moment because I was a young kid. I was different than those around me and some people noticed. He looked me straight in my eyes and spoke with a hoarse voice, "They were both killed. I don't know what else to say besides I'm sorry." He patted me on my shoulder and walked away. He left me standing there alone, in prison, and speechless.

I stood there for a few seconds but in my perception it was an eternity. I had nothing but doubt in my mind. His words didn't register. I didn't believe that God would allow the most important people in my life to be taken from me. That experience in my life was far more horrible to me than going to prison. I loved my parents more than life itself.

My heart shattered inside my body. I didn't know how I was still breathing. I felt like all I could do was exhale. Every time I tried to breathe, it was like trying to grab air as I was falling to my death. It was the most miserable I had ever felt my entire life. The conviction had no merit compared to how I felt then. All I knew, all I could think was in an instant, I was completely alone.

I trembled as I stepped back into my cell. I broke down right there on the floor. I couldn't keep a cover on all my bottled-up emotions. I was crying harder than I had ever before. I gasped for air after every yell of pure, endless agony. I tried to quit bawling but the pain was so high that my body didn't know how to cope. I didn't know what emotion to feel.

The feeling that surfaced the most was anger—pure, evil anger. Pure rage wrestled through my veins. I wanted to hurt someone, anyone. I wanted someone to feel how I was feeling. I felt betrayed by my parents. They left me there all alone. I felt betrayed by God. *How could God allow this to happen?* I had already been through a lifetime of pain in only a couple decades of life. It was enough.

I felt God was who I needed to blame because an all powerful being could have stopped it. He could have saved them but He didn't. It was His fault. A loving God wouldn't do that. I wanted to know why. I was disgusted with life. Everything had changed in such a short amount of time. It wasn't fair.

I felt like I was being tortured. I thought to myself, *At least death would be instant.* Now I had no family, no freedom. I had no life. I was completely abandoned on this earth. I thought about death. *Who would care about me?* I didn't know any of my extended family. I didn't think any were still alive. My mom had a sister but I had never developed a relationship with her.

Growing up, I had mom and dad. My parents had a ton of friends before the murder conviction but after I was convicted, people didn't know how to react. They didn't want to risk being around my family if I was actually a killer. I didn't blame them because they didn't know that I had literally nothing to do with the crime. They couldn't see through my eyes.

I lost all my friends too. Everyone I had growing up had left me after all that happened. I truly believe most didn't believe I did it but they still weren't there to support me. They weren't around when times got tough. I had my friends in prison but that was mostly Gabe. Jesse talked to me occasionally around the prison but he ran around with the gang crowd. I was hurting too much to think clearly.

Gabe turned and looked at me from up on his bunk. I was on the floor, curled in a ball, trying to contemplate what had just happened to my life. I looked up to see my only friend staring at me, his eyes had tears but he didn't say a word. I started to bawl even harder. My arms were trembling and I felt I was suffocating. Gabe jumped down and sat by me on the cold concrete floor. I leaned against the only person that cared for me in the entire world and cried until I passed out. Not one word was said that night, not even one.

I woke up for breakfast but didn't have the appetite to go. Gabe wasn't in the cell, so he must have left for breakfast without me. I was still in a surreal environment. I couldn't believe my parents were gone or I was in prison. I had to smack the concrete wall to ensure I felt something. I started to become angrier, even hateful. I hated the malicious prosecutor and the lying detectives that put an innocent kid in prison.

I hated that one of my greatest fears had come true. I was completely alone. I had nothing to look forward to. I was broken beyond repair. Worst of all, I hated God. I questioned everything about him. *How is God good? How could He let this happen to me? Is He a loving God? Why are my parents dead and I'm going to spend the rest of my life in prison?*

I didn't understand how God could allow me to lose everything and expect me to remain faithful. I couldn't think of one good part of my life. What value is health when I didn't want to be alive in the first place? I felt the darkness cover my heart. I had become hateful, like everyone around me. For the first time in prison, I fit in.

I looked up into the mirror above the sink. I saw a completely different person. When I saw myself, I knew I was done with God. I was done with who He was supposedly trying to make me. Everything that I had ever valued was stolen and I had enough. I wasn't going to spend my life serving a being that could allow such pain. I quit right then and there.

Chapter 9

I LIVED WITH THAT HATEFUL mindset for over a decade. I never got to attend my parent's funeral. It bothered me to an extent I can't explain. I never got closure. The thought of losing them haunted me every day and all it left me with was a hating heart.

I hated people and anyone that wanted a piece of me got it. I spent those years showing how tough I was or how tough I thought I was. I would beat people down both physically and verbally, anyone for any reason.

I was petty when it came to fighting. I remember punching a guy in his face for accidentally stepping on the back of my shoe. My temper rose to its peak instantly. I turned and swung without thinking. I smashed my fist into his jaw and he fell to the ground immediately. He didn't get up and retaliate. He looked up at me from the ground with shock. He couldn't believe that I would hit him because of a small accident.

He didn't realize that I could care less about my shoe. I swung at him because I was feeling hurt myself. When I would fight, it kept my mind off of how much I hurt inside. I learned to have as short of a fuse as possible. It was about the principle. If I didn't fight, I felt weak physically. I was already gone emotionally and spiritually, so I didn't want to lose physically too.

At the time I didn't realize that I was making life harder on myself. I lived for the instant gratification rather than looking at the impact my decisions would cause in my future. I never thought about the consequences of my violence. I blamed it on being a victim of my circumstances. Life made me this way so I had to get back at life. Even the Bible stated, "An eye for an eye." I justified the behavior by manipulating the Bible. I thought I had the right to repay hurt with hurt.

I affected more people than I knew. I stole from those who were trying to avoid violence by bringing it to them. They could be trying to run the straight and narrow, and I was the one who threw them off course. Most people on the yard had a substantial amount of time but if I ruined freedom for just one person then it was wrong. That was the viciousness of the devil's destruction. It was a domino effect, take a group of lives by starting with one life.

My most memorable brawl was one of my last. It wasn't one that I won either. Honestly, I believe nobody wins fights but someone does get less hurt. In this instance, I wasn't the one who got less hurt. The guy walked with confidence and didn't have any gang affiliations. He was an average inmate that never drew attention to himself. To top it all off, it was a one-on-one fight. But I learned quickly I bit off more than I could chew.

I remember it so vividly. It all started because I was a bully. His friend stepped in front of me as we were walking to chow. I called his friend out who was far smaller than me. The guy was fresh into prison and scared. I understood because I remembered what he was feeling. He backed down when I called him out. I felt so powerful. I thought I was strong but the truth was I knew I was weak.

After he backed down, his friend stepped up. I was instantly enraged because I felt disrespected. He was smaller than me too, but he acted completely different. He didn't look scared. I stared into his eyes with a nasty glare to try to intimidate him. He glared back and clinched his fists. He was pumped up and prepared to fight. He jerked his head back to get his long black hair out of his face. As his hair flew back behind his head, I noticed his eagle tattoo erupting out from the side his neck.

I was irritated and that quickly escalated to rage. I wanted to beat him down for making me feel disrespected so I attacked first and started swinging left, left, right. He was the quickest fighter I had ever fought. He dodged everything I sent his way. I was shocked that someone could move so swiftly and with such coordination. He hit me square in the jaw with pure power. I was angry but even more so, I was humbled.

There was a code in prison. Don't back down from anyone. He fought me because he was protecting his friend. It was honorable to stand up for the weak. I respected him for that but I had none for anyone else. Murderers came through the prison gates thinking they were tough and most got proven wrong by even more ruthless murderers.

The way I saw it was if anyone disrespected me then they were going to see a fury of fists. I wanted to establish dominance and to be able to back it up too. That was until I got humiliated. I was knocked down so fast I didn't know how to react. It was more of a blessing than anything else. After the fight, they put me into The Hole. It wasn't anything new. I was in and out of B-block all of the time.

That place was a different type of awful. I had a thin rubber mat and sink with one blanket and that's all. The lights were never on and they never let me out. I didn't have anything to read, watch, or do. The only way I kept my sanity was by taking the button off my shirt and trying to bounce it in my shoe. The meals they brought to me while I was in there were nothing but a bowl of some type of rotting slop. Most visits were two weeks but my longest was forty-two days. It depended on the damage of the fight that sent me there. They had no where else to send me. I was in the most violent, highest security institution they had in the state.

I seemed to be sent to the same cell every time I went back to The Hole. It was small and compact. I found it to be slightly cozy at the same time. I didn't like it for a while but I learned to enjoy it because it was so quiet. I didn't have any distractions. The air was unventilated. It made me feel like I was choking with every short breath.

Most people hated The Hole. I knew I didn't like it either but I was there so much I should have just stayed. I learned to like certain parts so I could keep my sanity. I liked how cool it stayed in the cell. Even in the heat of summer it still remained cool. The worst part was, in the cell I was always in, water constantly dripped from the sink.

The sound it made drove me absolutely insane. I would get so irritated that I would yell, scream, and pound on the door. I wanted to cause as much of a riot as I could. I could still make it miserable for the other inmates around me. All I wanted was for them to fix it. I remember yelling at the top of my lungs, "Fix the darn sink!" I wasn't as nice with my actual word choice but they would still respond with a nice smile and respond, "Deal with it."

It made me so angry that I would forget how disruptive I was. I yelled for hours on end until I got to the point where I broke. I had become so shattered by the loss of my parents that I didn't care about others. It was pure selfishness. I wanted everyone else to feel hurt so we would have something in common. I inflicted pain because of my emotional distress.

It took me being humbled to realize that I was the one making the wrong choices. That was no way to live. A life full of violence hurt me more than I realized. I let the devil get a foothold when I lost my parents. The Bible warned me of it but I lacked the maturity it took to notice. I had thought that I wanted to change but I didn't know how. I did know that the Lord was where I had to start. I felt I wanted to become a protector, not a perpetrator, but that type of thinking usually didn't last long.

Gabe would still be around when I would be sent back to general population. He was still my friend and was always polite to me even though I had turned into a very violent person. They would put me back in the same old cell with him every time I got out of The Hole. It didn't bother me though because even though I changed I still cared for Gabe.

Gabe stayed my cellmate the entire time I was on yard. I think they noticed that he was a positive person in my life or maybe it was just chance. He was the same way since day one. He was calm and collected. I truly felt he was the wisest man I had ever met. He would occasionally bring up the Bible in our conversations. Usually, I went back to my old ways after I got out of the hole. I would be very adamant about changing when I was away from everything but once I was back in the mix, I went back to my violent ways. It was a hard habit to break. I felt I wanted God but I thought it would make me look weak. So whenever Gabe would bring up God, I would still tell him to "Can it."

He would but I don't think it was because he was intimidated but because he was respectful. Gabe lived very simply. He had the same routine for ten years. He spent almost every day reading his books, jogging, and going to the chapel. He constantly worked on his mind, body, and spirit.

I didn't have a routine. I walked around looking for someone to antagonize. I sought for a battle and wanted to fight anyone for any reason. I had taken plenty of beatings but given even more. It felt like hurting was the only thing that made me happy. My heart was different compared to before. I had such an empty void. I was hurt so I coped with it the only way I felt I could.

I woke up early in the morning to get ready to walk to chow. Gabe was still sleeping soundly on his bunk. I walked over to the sink and washed my face. I looked up into the stainless steel mirror above our sink. I felt disgusted when I looked into my eyes. I wasn't the man I wanted to be. I still hadn't forgiven my parents for abandoning me, but I knew the path I was on was not mine to take. I thought to myself, *This isn't the son they would have wanted.*

I suddenly felt a blanket of calmness cover my mind. I felt tranquil and my being felt at peace. I closed my eyes as time stopped and I drifted into deep thought. I hadn't felt that way since my trial. I opened my eyes and couldn't quit staring at the man in the mirror. *Who was he?* It wasn't the man I thought I would become.

That moment was my rock bottom. I didn't want to live that way anymore. I didn't want to live for me anymore. I stared at myself with no idea what path was ahead of me. All I did know was the path

I was on was going to change direction. I did something I hadn't done in ten years—I prayed.

I closed my eyes. I had no feeling throughout my entire being. I felt like I was totally apart from my physical body. I felt so close to my soul. I felt so pure. I meditated on God and how forgiving He is. My thoughts consisted of nothing but God's perfection. His glory, power, and grace saturated my being. I felt like I was home again, like I belonged. My prayer was about my gratitude.

When I opened my eyes, I was back in reality. I didn't know how much time had passed but I don't imagine it was very much. Gabe was still in bed and breakfast had not been called. I started to think about that moment of bliss that had just occurred. It felt like it was a reminder that I was still capable of happiness. God was still there and had never left me. I wavered from Him, but He didn't waver from me. I didn't know where to start to get my life back on track but I knew that I was going to change. God was more important to me than I was to myself. I made Him a promise as I stood there. From that moment on, I would live for Him.

I think that was the point in my life where I felt I was truly saved. I felt that I sincerely gave my heart to God. I was truly born again because that old me was dead and gone. The old me that loved myself didn't exist. All I had left was the real me. He was the same man who would live for God. I wanted His will not mine. My mind transformed instantly as I gave everything I had to God.

"Chow!" The officer yelled into our tier.

I looked back at Gabe as he hopped off his bunk to go to breakfast with me. We started walking toward the chow hall to go eat. Gabe didn't say much as we walked but asked me an important question.

"There is a pastor coming from the outs today if you want to come?" I needed that invite. He couldn't have had better timing because if he had asked me the day before, I would have told him to screw off in a less polite term.

The morning went by at its usual pace. I told Gabe I would join him for chapel and I was going to keep my word. He grabbed his

Bible and I walked with him down to the church. On the walkway, he started to discuss how Jesus felt about the church from what he has read in the Bible. He talked about the importance that was put on fellowship and that was what church was all about.

We arrived at church and the guards patted us down as we entered. We both sat in the third row, near the middle of the section. The pastor was standing at the podium shuffling through his notes. Other inmates were walking in and finding their seats. I felt uncomfortable and didn't feel like staying, but I decided I would stay anyway. Gabe sat happily right next to me and then the sermon began.

"Good afternoon," the pastor said.

"I have an important message for all of you." He paused for a couple seconds and looked around the room. I assumed that he would look down on us in judgment but he looked at all of us with compassion. I could tell in the first few minutes of watching that he cared for us, even though we were inmates.

He looked around the room as he spoke, "Jesus loves you." He had a specific intensity in his eye. It was passion.

"I could finish right now and feel the most important sermon ever preached has already finished. But I do have another message prepared and I would hate for it to go to waste." Most inmates looked up at him with a smile on their face. I smiled too. This pastor had some wit and he caught my attention.

The chapel was bland and normal. It looked like most other rooms throughout the prison. It was bigger though and could fit at least a hundred inmates. It never had that type of attendance though. It had the typical wooden pews and plain white paint on the walls. The only color in the entire room was some flowers in a vase at the back. I didn't care what the chapel looked like. It would be nice if it seemed like I wasn't in prison while I was there but that simply wasn't reality. I had abandoned all thoughts of extravagance and accepted what I had.

I struggled to keep my focus off the pastor. He was a tall, slender man with a decent suit on. The part that drew my attention the most was the way he spoke. He was passionate and it made me interested in everything he had to say.

"I want everyone here that has their Bible to turn to the book of Matthew," he said. I heard some pages shuffling around me. I didn't bring a Bible so I sat quietly as everyone else found their spot. It didn't take much time before he spoke again.

"Now, let's read about the story of when Jesus walked on water."

He read the story and than started to paraphrase about what happened.

"So the disciples are sitting in the boat and they look out to see Jesus is walking to them. The disciples see Jesus and at first they think Jesus is a ghost, but Jesus says, 'It is I, I am real.' So Peter asks to walk to Jesus and Jesus tells him to come.

Now, pay close attention to this. Peter is focused on Jesus so he too is walking on water. Then suddenly Peter looks around and what happens—he starts to sink. Then he yells for Jesus to save him so Jesus reaches out and pulls him up."

I was interested in his message. I had heard and read that story for years. I was interested in hearing another way to interpret the story. I kept thinking to myself. *What does this guy have to add to it?* I have heard the, "all is possible with Christ" message before. *What new could he bring to the table?*

"Now, this is what I see from this story. When I look at this world, I imagine it as a spiritual ocean. Every spirit is in this ocean and Jesus our Lord and Savior walks on the top of the water." He stepped away from the podium and walked slightly toward the inmates.

"Now, stay with me." He looked around the room to ensure he had everyone's attention. "Some men are barely keeping their heads above water, some are just beneath the surface, some are on top of the water, and some have already drowned."

"Now, the ones who are walking on water are different then the ones just beneath the surface, how?" He looked around the room but no one gave him any feedback. "The men on the water are focused. They have their eyes on Jesus so it allows them to walk on water with Him. If they were to look down and lose focus, then they would also sink. Are you with me?" Most men around nodded their heads.

"It is important to be above the water because at that point, a fellow Christian can start lifting up other people. They can help each other out of the ocean to walk with Jesus. They could point and say, 'Look! There is Jesus. Focus on Him,' and then they could walk on water too. Then that pair of men can help others up and it would increase astronomically." He was smiling as he envisioned his statement.

"Now, what about the men under the water. What do they have to do?" A man at the front spoke up and said, "They have to reach out." The pastor smiled down at him and said, "Exactly."

"Now, picture it all in your head—an ocean so vast, full of people. Some men have drowned because they turned their back on God and they are gone. They have sunk to the bottom and you can not reach them. Then look at the amount of people that are reaching out everywhere. Now, the Christians with their focus on Jesus can be walking around on the water pulling all these people out to walk with Christ. What a vision I can see?

The key is the focus. If we take our eyes off Christ, we too will sink. If we keep our focus on Christ then look at what we could accomplish together. That is what I want you to take home today. I want you to look at yourself in the mirror. Where is your focus? If it is on Jesus, then start pulling people out of the ocean before they drown. The prison environment has a much rougher sea but men here are still reaching out. Go save them!"

I enjoyed the pastor's message. Gabe and I talked about how clever of an analogy that pastor had. Then we started to add to it and the fellowship began. We talked about how important it is to remain focused on the positive. Everything about that pastor's sermon was inspiring to me. I could see the plan he was trying to share with us. It was a neat vision to have and for the first time in a long time, I felt back to normal.

The fellowship was the turning point. It was good to have some-one to talk to when I had an angry thought. I could talk to Gabe and be real about what I was talking about. I could talk of the hurt I felt from the loss of everything I had ever loved. Gabe was still by my side and that feeling was unexplainable.

I felt like I was part of Christ's family again but at the same time I was never truly gone. God still loved me even when I was so hurt that I hated everyone, including Him. I felt free again, I was the prodigal son. I returned to Christ's family and was met with open arms. I wish I could explain how great that felt. It was so amazing to be at peace again. I have an infinite amount of gratitude for what Christ did and does for me.

Chapter 10

GABE HAD BEEN WITH ME for years. He had seen me turn my back on God and become the man I never wanted to be. He remained by my side even when I insulted him and God. I was so angry and trapped.

After that sermon, I became driven. I wanted to grow and get back to my roots. Gabe offered to have a Bible study together so we both could start practicing Christian principles together.

My anger at the world started to subside. I became content with what life had hit me with. Nothing had hit me as hard as life had. It seemed so wrong, so unfair. Growing up I never thought that I would be where I was, with what I had. I had literally nothing a day before. I had no freedom or family. I had nothing, not even the clothes on my back were mine.

But, on that day, I had something and it was my biggest treasure. I had my relationship with the Lord back. He never left me, even when I left Him. He let me choose my road for over a decade and He remained faithful. I am forever indebted to Him. He is everything to me, my Alpha and Omega, my beginning and end.

Over the next three years, I diligently studied the Lord's word. I practiced biblical principles to the best of my ability. Gabe and I had Bible studies daily and I could quote scripture left and right. The answer to any life problem was written somewhere in the Bible. Every trial or tribulation had a way out but only when I was looking.

Prison was exactly the same from the day I walked in. I was the one that had changed.

It was still very violent inside prison walls. I saw more than a dozen men lose their lives from brutal beatings. Mass gang wars and prison corruption were prevalent over the entire yard. Most guards were not much better than inmates. They smuggled in drugs for the gang members. They would even plant false evidence in cells to get rival gang leaders removed.

The best way to live was to avoid it. That lifestyle put many men in the grave and when I saw something that I shouldn't have, then I made sure no one else saw me see it. I couldn't risk becoming a loose end and being discarded.

I got out of the mix as much as I could. Out of sight, out of mind was my new lifestyle. I lived my life simply again. There were instances where I would have attacked a man before but I learned to turn the other cheek. God gave me eyes of grace to see through other's faults because I didn't know their stories. I don't know what happened in their lives to make them vicious, violent people. They could have a story like mine. It was never my place to judge from the beginning.

The homosexuality was still prevalent. Consensual or not, it still happened. I couldn't help those who choose to indulge in immorality and it wasn't my place to judge them either. Sin is sin. A liar is no better than a murderer or adulterer. We are all lost sheep.

I applied to the warden to start a class at the chapel for a weekly Bible study. Surprisingly, he approved of it and I was the instructor. I had to direct the class and keep it proper. I couldn't allow gang activity or violence to occur. Otherwise, he would ban the class. It was very difficult at first but as the class developed, so did the students. They only came because they wanted to learn about Christ. Gang members used other avenues to conduct their business.

It really occupied my time. Every week I had to come up with a different topic in the Bible, but honestly, I could have shown up, opened a page at random, and talked about any random verse. It was about God's glory and thinking about what has been done for us. It wasn't about having a perfect Bible study.

If I waited for perfect conditions and the perfect sermon, I wouldn't have made it anywhere. The church was for a body of people to worship together, not for the perfectly righteous to convene. I have never met a perfect person, so I doubt a church of perfect people would have any attendance at all.

Jesus came for the sinners, the lost sheep, which means he came for all humanity. He came with a promise that he will keep—that if you accept him as your Lord and Savior, then you shall have eternal life. I love what he did. I love that he was courageous enough to make that sacrifice. My gratitude surfaced from my soul and I was going to repay him to the best of my ability.

Gabe helped me with the Bible study on occasion. He never spoke but he did help me pick out topics to discuss. He also motivated me to keep the faith. He lived as an example to me and proved, regardless of the situation, there was always hope. I loved how Gabe chose to show me rather than tell me. It gave me a new perspective on what being a Christian actually meant.

After a couple months of Bible classes, a familiar face walked in through the door. It was Jesse. He walked in, sat down, and relaxed at the back of the class. We went through the hour and he didn't say anything, he just listened. I was okay with it because sometimes, I find it is better to simply listen to God's word when I have a heavy heart. I knew something was on his mind because I had only talked to him about a dozen times over the last ten years.

He had changed. He had joined the KPK when he arrived on the yard. The KPK stood for King Pin Killers and they were the head gang on the yard. Every dirty guard and drug had associations with them. They were ruthless. They were about loyalty and efficiency. The higher-ups or shot-callers took organized crime to a new level. They ran several illegal operations on the streets from inside of the prison. For the most part, they ran the prison itself.

There were a couple other gangs around the yard but they were trivial compared to the KPK. They didn't have the numbers or power. They didn't have the distinct hierarchy either. The KPK was a blood in, blood out type of unit. "Ride or die" was what they called it. It meant that to be part of the gang, blood was required and to get out, death was. It was a merciless operation and was based on account-ability. I had distaste for the KPK and all other gangs because of how they operated. It bothered me that they could destroy so blindly. Most deaths in the prison were gang-related, so were most fights. It was part of the environment and it was awful.

Jesse had put in over a decade of work for the KPK. That meant he lived according to their rules, doing whatever he was instructed to do. To me, that lifestyle was an illusion; they showed love but their loyalty was to the crew as a whole. It was all about the gang surviv-ing. An individual didn't actually matter and was expendable. It was a lifestyle for people who were searching for love. They wanted love so they killed to show it. I didn't understand that type of thinking.

Jesse's appearance was different. He had not aged very well. He had shaved his head and he looked like he had stressed a lot over the years. He had a lot of tattoos on his arms but I wasn't intimidated even with an appearance like he had. He was different around me compared to when he walked the yard. When he walked around the yard, he had to show a front of power and strength. When he was with me, he went back to his normal self—a broken, lost man search-ing to fill the void inside himself.

I knew when he stepped into the chapel that he had realized he wanted the Lord to run his life. I had tried in the first few years of knowing him to get him to commit to Christ, but at that time I had no success or the success I did have was simply planting the seed. Then I turned and wasn't a very good example. I believed my experi-ences could help him though. I knew both roads and could relate to the point he was at.

After class, Jesse came up to me. The other inmates had already walked out of the room and I was taking my time packing up my notes.

"That was a great class today," he said as he walked up to me.

"Yes, perseverance is essential to success," I replied.

"I'm sure you're curious why a gang banger like me is coming up in your class." I shook my head from side to side. I knew what he wanted. Otherwise, he wouldn't have come to the chapel in the first place.

"No, not really, but I'm glad you came."

He walked closer to me and sat down in a chair. I set down all my notes to pay him more attention. He crossed his arms and leaned back in the chair to get more comfortable.

"Well, the truth is, I'm up for release in eleven months and I don't want to live this life anymore. I don't want to be slinging dope or hurting anyone. I just, you know, want to be a good person and be happy again and stuff. I'm over everything here. You know, I want to be a better person and have a family when I get out. I got mad love for my brothers still, but I want to do me."

I was nodding as I listened to him. I thought back to when the pastor told me that people have to reach out to be picked up out of the ocean. That pastor showed wisdom in what he said because that was exactly what Jesse was doing. It was funny how God would work sometimes. I wanted to go out and spread the gospel everywhere around me, but God brought His lost sheep straight to me. I found it ironic, but I was still thankful that Jesse had eager ears.

"I understand," I said and started walking toward the door with Jesse.

"How about next week you come back and we can teach you more about God's word?" He smiled but didn't show any of his teeth.

"Alright, but Luke, do not let any of my homies know I'm coming here. They don't like stuff that doesn't have to do with the gang, you know." I smiled and nodded my head as he walked out of the room in front of me.

Over the next six months, Jesse came to the Bible study pretty constantly. He actually participated too, but out on the yard he still had his tough guy cloak on. In class, he was knowledgeable and polite, but anywhere else he had to represent the KPK. Our class remained quite small but the men attending were trustworthy. The men loved the Lord so they never worried about each other's business out on the yard. We all did our own time and it worked out best that way.

Jesse walked into the Bible study as usual. We went through talking about the story of Joseph and him being falsely accused and sent to prison. We talked and related points in our own lives. We concluded sometimes life wasn't very fair. The class went really well and we ended in prayer.

After class, Jesse came up to me and said, "Luke, I don't know what is going to happen in my life over the next few days."

I looked at him curiously, "What do you mean?"

He was frantic when he spoke. "Well, I have been praying a lot and stuff. I did what I felt I had to do and I dropped out of the KPK. I was asked to take care of a guy and I just couldn't do it. I don't want to live that way anymore. They looked at me as weak because I wouldn't kill him. I think they were trying to make sure I didn't go home. The head boss wants me to stay and do business here on the yard. So if I kill and get caught then I won't leave. You see what I mean?"

"Well, this is a dilemma. I have been here a while and we both know that dropouts aren't tolerated. This may be a time to get off the yard," I replied.

He looked at me with pride in his eyes. "I can't do that. I won't live scared of people. I'm not afraid of them."

I didn't know how to respond to him. He had dropped out of the top gang on the yard. They had a lot of power throughout the prison. The thing about it though was Jesse was higher-up than a prospect. It always ended with blood when someone like that tried to walk. They would make an example out of him. All the founders were killers doing life and then some. They wouldn't hesitate to green light him, which is slang for put out a hit. But even if he wasn't scared for his life, I was.

"Well, what do you think we should do? Maybe you should go into protective custody. You're free in a couple of months and your pride isn't worth your life," I said.

He put his head down slightly for a moment, then looked up and said, "No, I will not run from this. My entire life I have spent running from my problems. I always regretted the times where I was a coward. I hated when I ran and I don't want that. I never stepped up when life was hard and I'm going to change that. Even if I do run, they will still come, they won't quit." I looked back at him.

"This is different though, this is your life. This may not be the best battle to choose. Fight the good fight. Remember." He started to pace back and fourth in front of me with his hands on his head. He took his time before he spoke.

"No, this is my battle. I'm thankful for you, Luke. Over the last few months, I found God again. I know what path I want to live. It's a path for God. He will direct my steps. I probably wouldn't have changed if it wasn't for this. It's just a class but I have learned a lot. Promise me that you won't tell the guards. I have to stand up for myself."

I was hesitant and didn't know what to do but I replied, "I promise." I sighed after the words left my mouth but I wasn't going to break my promise to him. I gave him my word and in prison that's important to keep.

I looked back up at Jesse and said, "Meet me at the library tomorrow at ten. I know that there are more options and we'll figure something out." He nodded his head and walked out of the room. I didn't like the way I was feeling about the situation. It was awful.

Everyone had left the Bible study. I stayed in the chapel to think. I didn't know how to help Jesse. He was in an awful situation. I had seen from experience what the KPK was capable of. I was afraid for his life. I dropped to my knees and prayed for God to take the power away from the evil in the prison. I didn't want the KPK to have the say in what happens to Jesse's life. He was a good man and had developed into a great friend.

He was the first friend I had made and it carried with us over the years. It was a different type of friendship. We didn't have to spend time with each other or talk. We simply had a mutual respect for each other. I knew if I ever needed anything, he would help me. It was easy and natural for us to get along. He was too important for me to let anyone hurt him. I was prepared for battle.

Chapter 11

I WAS BACK IN THE cell and I told Gabe the situation involving Jesse. He didn't say much about it besides that his safety was very much at risk. I wanted to tell the guards so they would ship him into a protective custody unit but I couldn't. Jesse was almost a free man. *Why would he risk everything?* Especially risk it for something as petty as pride.

We both knew they would go after him. They wouldn't stop and they would hurt him. I knew that his best option would be to stay out of the mix. He had to leave general population. They would find him in his cell or around the yard. All he had to do was survive a few months but I couldn't make him enter protective custody. I was completely conflicted.

I was pacing around the cell thinking of how I could help protect him. They had numbers and resources. They were killers and I wasn't. I was strong but not against a large group of murderers. I want to see good happen in his life. He had transformed so much from the first day he stepped into the chapel. Jesse had grown in his wisdom and knowledge. He made plenty of bad decisions but he still found his way home to the house of the Lord. He has been forgiven and I would hate for everything to end badly.

Morning came around and I headed to breakfast. I usually saw Jesse when I went to chow because his unit finished eating as mine began. I walked into the chow hall and he was in there. Something was up though. He was sitting at a table with his back toward the wall and his head on a swivel. I recognized several of his ex-affiliates sitting at the table across from him.

One of the founders stood up. He was well-known around the yard. His name was Cyrus Black but around the yard most called him "Black." He was bald and stalky with tattoos down his left forearm. He also had a tattoo of three black bars on his face. They were directly under the outside of his right eye. They were a symbol of his rank in his gang. It meant he was one of the founding three.

He was a racist, street thug before he got to prison. He only got worse after he tasted the hate circulating throughout the prison. From what I heard, he was convicted of shooting two black men for no other reason than because they were black. He killed them as they were walking down the side of the street.

It turned out that they were actually members of a Christian church. They were missionaries going from door-to-door, handing out Bibles and spreading the gospel. I instantly didn't like him because of why he was in prison but I never interacted with him either. He was a founder of the KPK and I had no business with him.

He started to walk toward Jesse and my heart dropped. He said something to him as he was walking up. I started to step toward him in case something happened. Jesse stood up as the leader reached out his hand to shake it. I was shocked. I didn't know what had happened. They grabbed hands and the leader reached around and embraced him. I felt so much relief. Something must have happened. I thought, *Maybe they are going to let him walk free.*

Suddenly I saw something glistening in Cyrus's hand. My legs went stiff and heavy. I tried to move toward him. I started to yell as he drew back the sharp piece of metal in his hand. "Je—!" was all I got out before he brutally started stabbing him in the back of the neck and spine. Time stopped, I couldn't believe what my eyes were showing me. I wanted to help but the shock rustling through my veins caused my body to seize.

All I could do was watch. Every blow of swift, endless power caused me to clench my teeth. I couldn't believe my friend was being stolen right in front of my eyes. It was gruesome and disgusting. I felt helpless; I was helpless.

In an instant, the guards immerged out of nowhere and tackled Cyrus to the ground. The shank went flying from his hand as he impacted the concrete. They were all covered in blood. I couldn't count how many times I saw Cyrus swing before the guards got there. It was all one blur.

It happened so quickly. I wanted to react but everything was over before I knew it. Several guards were restraining Cyrus. The rest of the KPK members had crooked smiles across their faces. I couldn't understand what they were thinking. They were smiling at a man losing his life and proud of the man who took it. The next sight I saw was Jesse. He was on the ground in an awkward position. The puddle of blood was spreading away from his body. He was simply lying there in a pool of blood, motionless, lifeless.

That day was one of the longest days I ever had. I was mad at myself because I couldn't do anything to help or save him. I wanted to go back and change everything. I would go back and tell the guards to put him in protective custody. I should have anyway but at the moment I wanted to honor my friend's request. I couldn't help but think it was my fault.

His attack came faster than I thought it would. I thought it would take some time for him to become green lighted. I was wrong. It happened quickly and I wasn't ready for it. I talked to Gabe and he told me that it was in God's will and to trust God always. I was livid that it happened like it did. He was a good man and he died because he stood up for what he had believed in. He wanted to change into a better man and he did. At that moment, I realized how much Jesse had actually taught me. He showed me true honor has a price.

I thought of a quote that my dad used to tell me. "What's the difference between courage and stupidity? The outcome." I thought of the outcome that Jesse had. He had a unique outcome because he could be viewed as both courageous and stupid. He knew he would die and he stood there anyway as the man stole his life. In a way, I would say he gave them his life. It was a new way of turning the other cheek or giving the coat off his back. I guess for him it wasn't about fighting because he had already won. I realized I was more of the student than I had thought.

I started to think about Paul and the disciples. I thought about how much they had to go through with the hurt and loss back then. Then I thought of Jesus and the crucifixion. I started to break down, my heart was pounding and I wanted to bawl. My life was an example of loss and hurt. It started with me and made its way to Jesse. I sat down on my cell floor by myself.

I wanted to think about my struggles. I reanalyzed why I was fighting. I knew the majority of why I lived the way I did was because the gratitude of what Jesus did. He was my light and example. He taught me a different route to living. I knew Jesse was experiencing God's eternal glory and that helped. I knew from experience that when tragedy hit I had only two options—push God away or lean on Him. I had been down the wrong road before so I didn't want to take that route again. I chose to sit on that hard floor and pray. It was all I could do to comfort my shattered soul.

Weeks went by and I tried to cope with what happened by acting normal. I still had the Bible study class and that helped. It also helped when I talked to Gabe about all the hurt I felt. Gabe was really helpful and supportive. He wasn't around Jesse much but he hurt because I did. Black was put into segregation after the murder and he would stay there for a long time. I put one foot in front of the other. I was trying my best to get over the loss of my friend.

I did more soul-searching. I constantly asked myself questions like, *What's the point and is this worth the pain"* I could think back to when I lost my parents and the feelings were similar, but this time I didn't turn my back on God. This time was different. Instead of being mad at God, I leaned on Him more than ever before. My heart was aching and I truly needed Him every day, for every situation. I decided that I wanted to reach out to more people. I want to touch more people's lives in honor of my friend, my parents, and especially, for my love of God.

I went home with a smile on my face for the first time in awhile. I sat on my desk and talked to Gabe, asking what I could do to give back to who I loved most. He was excited about my enthusiasm and said, "I've wanted to tell you for awhile now but was waiting for when you were ready. I think you should start preaching. I see how well you do in the study and really think your story could inspire people."

I was ecstatic that Gabe believed in me enough to push me to preach. I could speak in front of ten guys that I was really comfortable with, but in front of eighty or more would be different. It was terrifying to me. I found it ironic that I didn't fear a murderer but I had stage fright. I felt humbled thinking of it and then went right back to scripture. *I can do all things through Christ who gives me strength.*

Making the decision to get out of my comfort zone was a really humbling experience. The truth was it was never about me. I wanted to preach for the glory of God. I wanted to share my testimony and life trials to men that may be going through the same thing.

I knew how hard life could hit. I lost my parents, my friend, myself, and my freedom in my lifetime. I never lost God though and I don't have the words to explain what that feels like. I would want to say serenity, bliss, heavenly, but those words won't give it justice. The words I look for when I think of God are not in the English vocabulary. It's because we truly can't comprehend how perfect He really is.

I started taking the steps to get in front of the altar. We had pastors come into the prison a couple times a week to preach to the inmates and inspire them to change their ways. I talked to several of them about being able to preach. I told them I had conducted a Bible study for several years and that I wanted to branch out to a bigger percentage of the prison population.

Several of the pastors listened to me and were pushing for me to succeed. They decided to give me a shot in front of a small fellowship of Christian inmates that had been there even longer than me.

I was ecstatic and really wanted to do well. I spent hours preparing. It took me a long time to decide what to preach about. I wanted to be clever and witty, but at the same time I wanted to be real. I knew how important it was to have hope. I knew that God's word shared a lot of hope so I decided to preach of it.

For the first time in my life, I felt I could do something great with my life. I struggled because the fear of failure kept me trapped. I would pray for courage and the most beautiful part was how often it was granted. I wanted to promote God's glory. It was the biggest reason why I decided to preach. Other than that was because I wanted change for myself. I wanted to break the barriers that I had set for myself.

I couldn't leave the physical prison but God freed me mentally. He opened my mind and encouraged me. He picked me up off the ground and showed me the life he had planned for me was better than the one I planned for myself. I truly believed His will was greater than my own and at that point I was finally going to start living.

I kept my sermon short. It was my first time behind the pulpit, preaching to a large crowd. I wanted to talk about my feelings of heaven and God. I wanted to speak to them about hope, why I believed the Bible, and why I accepted Christ. I still wanted to relate it to something that we were all familiar with.

I remember walking up to the front of the room before it started. I was so nervous that it felt like the butterflies in my stomach could have flown me out of the place. I felt calmer the closer I got though. With every step, the fears started to evaporate from my body. I knew I was walking the right path and ironically it was literally to the altar.

I stepped up the few stairs that led to the stage. I was calm and excited at the same time. I stepped behind the pulpit and stared down at its simple wooden top. I brushed the right side with the palm of my hand. If I was a cowboy, it was my horse, and I was ready to ride. It was a beautiful chapter in my life. I looked around the room at the different types of men sitting on the pews. Everyone was dressed the same as me. We all had our prison blues on, which were blue jeans and light blue button up shirts.

Everyone seemed to be calm. Their faces were bland and they were patiently waiting for me to speak. I was confident because I knew I was always supposed to be at that place at that time. It was no surprise to God's plan.

I started with the simple saying, "God is great." Several of the men sitting out on the benches politely nodded their heads. I knew at that moment that regardless of whether the sermon was life changing or not, I was doing it for God and that was all that mattered. It wasn't about me and I was thankful for that because if it would have been about me, I wouldn't have had the courage to attempt it. I would have justified sitting the sidelines like most people do their entire lives.

"I want to speak about something we all relate with. We hear enough about it as is but I want to speak about prison. We all know prison isn't an easy place to live in. Sometimes, the reality of what it's like is hard to depict in words. The violence and corruption comes hand in hand, but the truth is that isn't the worst part of it.

It's the feeling and fear of being alone. The guards don't care about the inmates and this is just a job to them. They don't know the story of our lives and don't care. So we can't take comfort in the guards. Inmates can be just as unreliable. I have found I can take comfort in only one thing—Jesus Christ.

Life in prison is tough. It is constant torture and the end feels out of sight most of the time. The days seem the same so it feels like constant, unending agony. It's like watching a boring, torturous movie. It plays over and over again for a life time. That's what causes the violence for the most part. The people become so bored that they fight so they have something new to talk about for the week.

This is something most of us already know. But I want to turn this back to humanity as a whole. I believe humanity itself is in a prison and they don't realize it. It's because they know nothing different. The same metaphor could be used if a woman was to have her baby on a deserted island and the child was raised there. Would that kid worry about his career? I doubt it because he wouldn't know what that was. He wouldn't know anything other than the environment he was raised in, so what would he have to miss?

That's how I feel about us here on earth, rather than in heaven. We don't understand it and we don't have the vocabulary to explain it, but the same could be related to the boy on the island. The outside world is still there whether he believed it or not. The same goes for believers and unbelievers. Whether we choose to give our life for Christ or not doesn't determine if God is real or not.

Some people know God is real because they have seen his works and felt his presence. The scripture says, "Look to the birds in the sky." The advanced development of a bird alone is proof of a creator. It would be like treasures washing ashore to that boy. All the clues of an outside world are there. Just as we get clues to the existence of God.

God shows proof to men. We just have to gain the perspective to notice. He's constantly letting treasures wash upon our personal shores, from the beauty of the landscape to the endlessness of the universe. We just have to believe and set sail to find what we have been missing. The best part is God is always there with embracing, loving arms waiting patiently for us to turn to Him."

A couple of the men were looking at me as if they were unsure of my opening to my sermon. It caused my confidence to drop dramatically. I wanted my sermon to be really good but at that instant, the only thought that crossed my mind was humility. I wanted to get in front of people and tell them how good God is. I honestly didn't worry about if it was a life changing sermon or not, but I was trying my best. I wanted to let God's glory show. I wanted all of us to be able to relate to each other so I picked something that I knew we could all understand.

My messages were—God is real, heaven is unimaginably great, and love the Lord. That was the impact my heart wanted to show others. I wanted to spread the gospel and tell people that Christ came and died for our sins.

After the sermon was over, I stepped down and a man walked up to me. He was clean cut with bright white hair combed over the top of his head. He was very old and looked fragile. I had never met or even seen him before. He was polite and walked up to talk to me. His voice was soft and mellow.

"Great job up there. I really like the perspective you had in your sermon today. I have been here forty-seven years and I can't say I ever thought of being born here. It would be the same whether I was born on an island or born in prison. I liked it; it was unique. You did very well and I wanted to thank you.

Anyway, I gave my life to Christ before you were born and I've had a lot of experiences in my life. It helps me see that you have a lot of potential. So I'll encourage you to keep pushing. You're doing great and remember God is great, always. He'll direct your steps."

"Thank you. I really appreciate your encouragement," I said with a simple smile. He nodded at me and had a grin covering his face.

"God bless," he said as he slowly walked away.

That was the first and last time I saw that old man. I found out later that he had died that same night in his sleep. He lived just long enough to listen to my first sermon but experience his last. It made me value my first sermon even more than before. It was the last time he heard someone promote the glory of God. I felt honored it was me. It helped that he took the time to encourage me. He was graceful as he approached and I saw a good man even though I didn't get to know him. I could see goodness radiate from his body and in my last days, I wanted to have the same influence with the people around me.

His simple gesture of encouragement gave me the drive to continue preaching, even when times got tough. It helped me stay focused and I believed at least one person would be influenced every time I preached. For me, one was enough. In fact, if I had to go through a life of turmoil to impact only one person, then my life of pain would be worth it. I would sacrifice my entire life for that one person. If that is what it took for that one to be saved then the cost was cheap. What is my life worth compared to the eternity of another? Eternity is obviously far more valuable.

Chapter 12

OVER THE NEXT SIX MONTHS or so, life went by pretty typically. I was allowed to preach once a month in front of about eighty to a hundred of the calmer inmates. The inmates who went to church had a lot better attitudes than the rest of the prison population. There wasn't as much of the prison mentality in the chapel, not much fighting or violence. It was one of the few places where we could all feel normal.

The majority of the church-going population was older as well, with the exception of a few. I enjoyed my life in the chapel. I felt I was living a valuable life and I accepted that it was all my life was going to be. At the same time, I was proud. I learned sometimes God has to send a man into the lion's den to simply calm the lions. I was honestly honored that he chose me.

The days were routine but the prison was a little calmer since Cyrus was moved to segregation. Others stepped up into his place but it wasn't the same. He was a different level of evil. I was glad that it was difficult to replace his wicked heart. I enjoyed knowing his unique insanity was no longer on the yard.

Gabe and I started to have even more in-depth conversations as the years went by. We knew each other so well that we could practically know what each other was thinking. I loved the man. He was my brother and the only consistent person in my life. He was supportive of my decisions and honest enough to steer me right when I was wrong. It was nice to know I still had someone who cared about me.

It was difficult to lose everyone in the outside world. I struggled with it for years.

I hadn't got a phone call or even a letter since my parents died. My universe was completely inside concrete walls. Even with all that, I was thankful for how my life did turn out. I wouldn't have become the man I was without it.

I remember the exact day. It was a Tuesday afternoon and Gabe was sitting at the desk drawing. I was on my bunk next to him preparing my sermon for the upcoming Sunday. The new tier sergeant stepped into view for the first time. He was walking around with another guard inspecting the unit. I could tell at first glance he was by-the-book. His posture was flawless and every step he took gave me the impression he had a military background.

I was curious about him because he was something new. It wasn't common to get a new tier sergeant. I watched him for a while as he casually strolled around peering into the cells. The first time I saw his face, I noticed a very angry look.

He looked down at everyone or more like he glared down at everyone. He wasn't very old, especially for a sergeant. He had blonde hair with long sideburns that grew into his beard. His attitude was his most obvious trait. He reeked of arrogance, but I didn't think much of him. I had run into plenty of proud people in my life, so they were nothing new to me.

Pride was one of my most hated character flaws. It bothered me because the self-righteous were the best at turning people away from God. I saw time and time again broken men going to the church for help, only to get kicked while they're down. It seemed to only come from people who thought they were better because they didn't make the same mistakes. It was a flaw in that specific person, not the church. The right church will love the sinner, not the sin.

After a few minutes of peering around, the sergeant made his way to the front of the tier.

"Standing count!" He yelled.

I stopped reading my Bible and stood up off my bunk. I walked up to the cold iron bars with my Bible in my hand. The new sergeant walked up to every door as he was counting the inmates and getting familiar with our faces. When he got to me, he looked me up and down with a face of disgust. He continued walking but didn't give any of the other inmates that look.

I turned and asked Gabe, "What was that all about?"

"That man probably has personal issues," he said calmly as he was climbing back on his bunk. I sat back down on my bunk feeling a little confused why that man had shunned me. *What did I do to him?* All he did was look at me. I never spoke to him or gave him an evil glare. I was confused by what I could have done to rub him wrong. I set my Bible down next to me as I began to think. I dissected everything I did in the short time he was there.

It was a different experience. Most guards didn't act that way. They were only trying to do their jobs. They tried to keep the majority of the population safe to the best of their ability. They really didn't give me a lot of grief ever since I quit fighting people. I was under the radar for the most part and like us, they just wanted to get through the day.

The sergeant was different. It was like he had a bone to pick with me. I could tell something had happened in his life to cause him to become angry, but why with me? I looked over at the Bible next to me and the thought hit me. *I get it. That man is really angry at God.* He must have seen the Bible in my hand during count.

I wanted to fix the problem. I wanted to help the man so I walked up to him to introduce myself. I thought kindness could change his perspective of me. Maybe I could show him that good people can be in bad places. Before I got there, he spotted me.

"What do you want, Bible thumper?" He said. I was drawn back and not ready for the instant insult. I stuttered some words as I tried to compose my thoughts.

I managed to say, "Just wanted to introduce myself."

He glared at me, "I don't need any new friends. Go back to your cell."

That battle felt lost so I calmly turned and headed home. I didn't look back at him or give him any more attention. It was enough for the day. I tried to approach him and plant the seed, but it didn't always work the first try.

Over the next couple of weeks, I stayed at a distance from Sergeant Woods. He made it blatantly obvious that he didn't like me or want anything to do with what I stood for. To him, I was just an inmate or lost cause. I felt so drawn to help him though. Sometimes, I saw men who denied God and there was nothing I could do, but I felt like his denial was a front. I finally managed to get enough courage to approach him again. I knew that all I had to do was try and God would take care of the rest.

I walked up to him as he was passing my cell. I felt certain I could show him that God was there regardless of his past tribulations. As I walked up, I was thinking and praying about what to say to him. I wanted to say something with such power that he would realize that living with hate in his heart was not living at all.

I walked up with my Bible snug against my body. I looked him directly in the eye and said, "Jesus loves you."

His eyes lit up and his face turned red as he gritted his teeth. I was stunned by his look of instant aggression. I had never seen that type of look in a man's face before. He responded with anger.

"God? There is no God. That is what pathetic, little people believe in so they can get the focus off of realizing they are a failure. They put hope in a make believe spirit so they can justify hardship. The truth is they are weak."

I was honestly more prepared for his reaction than I thought I would be. I stayed calm and had grown accustomed to men rebuking God with an insult. I wasn't going to fight with him or pressure his beliefs. My plan was to show him the door and let him know it's open if he wanted to enter. I had a calm, half-smile on my face as I listened to him. I turned serious instantly, "God is real; even more real than the concrete I walk on or those cinder block walls."

He didn't like that I responded to his statement. I think he thought I would hang my head and walk away. God didn't make me a push over and he made me passionate about Him. So naturally, I responded that his insult was inaccurate.

Seconds after I responded, his face flourished even more red and he grabbed me. He pulled my face only a couple inches from his and spit directly in my eyes. I bent over as I wiped my face and he hit me in my upper thigh with his baton. I fell slightly to the ground and he picked me up by the arm and threw me in my cell. I stumbled as I tried to catch my balance and I hit my face in between the metal desk and concrete wall. Blood started gushing out of my nose.

The sergeant slammed my door shut. He shouted into my cell, "How does a God exist that can let an innocent mother and child die in a fire? My boy was nine and his life was stripped. How can a good God let that happen? A good God wouldn't do that. He can't be real. There is no God!"

Gabe didn't do anything when the guard attacked me but what could he do? I was bleeding profusely from a small gash in my eyebrow and my nose. I turned and sat up with my back against the concrete wall. Gabe jumped down and handed me a wet towel that I pressed against my head to stop the bleeding.

I didn't get through to him at all but at least I learned why he turned his back on God. The ironic part was his story sounded dreadfully familiar. I remember exactly what emotions he was going through. It was hurt and sadness inside, but he showed rage. I prayed that it wouldn't take him a decade to realize God didn't do that to him. I was thankful that God would be infinitely patient and I believed I was put in his life for a reason.

The next morning, I woke up as they called chow, but my door never opened. All the other inmates took off toward the chow hall but we were still trapped in our cell. Sergeant Woods walked in front of the cell and peered in.

"Hope you're not hungry," he said with a devious face.

He walked away with a chuckle. I was not happy at all. I looked up at Gabe as he looked back at me.

"I'm not hungry anyway," Gabe said as he climbed back into bed.

I knew we both didn't like missing a meal. They were tiny to begin with and I knew we would both be hungry soon. The other inmates came back but our door remained locked. Everyone else went on with a typical day, but Gabe and I waited patiently in our cell. Nothing changed all day long, no lunch or dinner—nothing. I was starving as the day came to an end.

I was hoping it wouldn't happen again. The next day, I had to teach my weekly Bible study, so I really didn't want to get locked down. Most people would find it inhuman to lock a person down without food for a day, but a lot went on in prison that was cruel. I couldn't do anything to change it. The guard's word would take precedence over mine. I could try to sue or something, but then the target on my back would only be magnified.

Morning came around after that long day of hunger and suffering. The door opened at morning and I was relieved. Gabe and I put on our jackets and headed to the cell door when the Sergeant suddenly stepped in front of us. He had a tray of scraps from yesterday's breakfast. It looked like it had been left out all day. He dropped it on the ground inside of our cell and most of the food fell off the tray. It hit the ground and he smiled. He backed up out of our cell and closed the door.

"I hope you learn fast," he said as he walked away.

I was so hungry that I didn't really care that the food was dirty. It was a small portion of food and we both had to eat. We split the meal evenly and got as much off the ground as we could. I was starving but my body still knew that it tasted disgusting. I needed the nutrition so I forced it down. That day was just like the last, Gabe and I remained trapped. I missed my class for the first time ever. I was beginning to grow angry but something told me that kindness was the answer.

I was amazed at how content Gabe was. He spent his entire day in that cell happy as if it was a gift. He wasn't mad at Sergeant Woods. He spent his day reading and laughing. It inspired me. The thought crossed my mind, *What can man do to me?*

I was confined, hungry, and despised by the commanding officer. It was not a good experience to go through. An entire week went by and I was served only three very small meals. To top it off, we had to share. It was a hundred times more miserable than just being locked in The Hole. In this situation, I was constantly waiting to be fed. Time was slow and miserable.

At the end of the week, Sergeant Woods walked up and asked if I had learned my lesson. I didn't respond, no nod of agreement or disagreement. What was my lesson supposed to be? To accept there is no God would be to lie to myself. I would have rather starved than to have let him break me. I knew God was with me keeping me content in that cell, even if I didn't see Him. I wanted to be angry but God taught me how to be patient a long time ago.

Sergeant Woods snickered at me when I didn't respond. He smiled and walked away. The rest of the day went by normally and I made it over to the chapel for a service that night. Gabe came with me and when we got back our cell had been destroyed.

The mattresses and sheets were on the floor. All my other belongings were spread throughout the cell. Then I turned my view to the toilet. My pillow was a urine-soaked mess stuck in the bowl. I was frustrated that he would be so immature. Then my focus changed to the worst part. My Bible was shredded and scattered. Pages were torn to little bits and thrown everywhere.

Even the cover was almost unrecognizable. I was furious as I hit my knees. Even more, I was hurt and broken. I wanted to break down and cry. He had no idea how much my personal Bible meant to me. The book was my friend. It had spent a great deal of time with me. I had notes written throughout it and it felt as it was part of me. It was an extension of who I was as a person. It had comforted me when I was sad and encouraged me when I was down. I had read from it every day for years.

I was instantly mad at myself for not taking it with me, but I left it there so it would be safe. I never would have predicted that this would have happened. I was struggling to hold back my emotions. Messing with my Bible was like messing with my family. I wanted vengeance and was thinking of revenge when the thought hit me, *He can't take God's word from me."*

I was right. It was a perfect time to live by what the Bible says. The Bible is awesome and I love it, but what it is about he can never destroy. He couldn't take God's word. It was imprinted in my mind. I had the entire thing nearly memorized. He ripped up the pages but could take nothing that I didn't give him. I decided to forgive him quickly and take it as a lesson learned. I felt uplifted as I forgave him. I knew I was walking the right path. I did the only thing I could at that moment—I cleaned up my cell.

Chapter 13

OVER THE NEXT YEAR, I was targeted by Sergeant Woods. I made the decision that regardless of what he did to me, I was going to persevere and show kindness. That was what my heart told me to do. Several times I wanted to blow up and attack him for what he did. I couldn't get any more time than life, so an assault of an officer wouldn't do much. But to me that was what mercy was.

I had the ability to do something and chose not to, it's a lot different than not doing something because I couldn't. It was like the mercy Christ showed man when he was crucified. He could have ended all humanity but he showed mercy. I wanted to be a merciful man, not one that responded with an eye for an eye. It was difficult to think differently than those around me. It was hard to be a Christian example, but I would rather suffer for being in Christ than triumph for being out.

My cell getting tossed when I returned from dinner or church was common. I was amazed the most by Gabe though. He hadn't done anything at all. He never spoke to the Sergeant Woods, yet he suffered right there with me. It reminded me of how God must feel when we suffer. I'm sure He too is by our side. He is being patient through hardship with us and wants a future of hope and happiness for us. It is an amazing thought that I am very thankful for.

All the torment from Sergeant Woods eventually started to subside. I knew he was becoming bored because I never reacted to his attacks. I leaned on God to help me through the tough times. I never hated him even though at moments it was very hard to do so. One of the toughest accomplishments as a Christian was to learn to love the unlovable.

It was also one of the most important parts of being a Christian. God is love and in order to act in his image, we too must love each other. It took God to get to the point where I could but it wasn't easy. I remember the day it all came to an end.

He strutted into my cell and instantly started crying. Gabe must have been at church or something, but he wasn't there. I was shocked and didn't know what was going on. He looked into my eyes before he spluttered out, "I'm sorry." After an entire year of damage, physically and emotionally, he walked into my cell as just another broken man.

"I went back to church for the first time in four years yesterday," he said.

I was still shocked that he had barged into my cell and immediately opened up.

"Susan would have wanted it. She was my high school sweetheart and I married her right after graduation. I loved her so much and she blessed me with my beautiful baby boy. I will always miss them so much."

He was crying pretty heavily at that time. I wanted to comfort him but I wasn't sure how to approach it. I decided to stay calm and listen. He took a couple minutes to calm down. He began to speak again in a sincere, delicate voice.

"I remember his first laugh, steps, smile, everything. I melted the first time I saw my little boy. He had no worries, just love. I loved watching him grow up. It was my favorite part of life. I want to go back and watch another one of his tee ball games. He was a great kid and my wife was a treasure too.

Susan always ensured we made it to church and she was the most loving person I knew. After the accident happened, I couldn't handle it anymore. My life was over. I was broken and shattered beyond repair. I turned to alcohol to cope. I couldn't manage anything in my life. I cried every time I drove past our old church because I hated anything that reminded me of the pain."

I felt as if I was looking in a mirror, not physically, but emotionally. The brokenness was so familiar it hurt. I remember exactly how it felt to be in his shoes. The all-is-lost moment or the lack of will to live has destroyed many men in the past. It would be easy to fall victim to the devil's destruction, but with God we will make it through any storm. He had his head tilted toward the floor as he was speaking to me.

"I turned after the accident. I moved here to get away from the past. I couldn't believe that God could allow this to happen to me. Susan loved the Lord and Jake was being raised in a Christian home. Susan and I strongly believed in the Scripture. For me and my family, we shall live for the Lord. Why would God do this? I miss my boy and want him back. He was stolen so early.

It's so hard. I can see them being burned, screaming for daddy to save them and I wasn't home. I can picture it and I see it in my nightmares. The worst part is I wasn't there when they needed me most. It haunts me everyday and not a day goes by that I don't think of them."

I empathized with what had happened. I remember what it was like and what I thought when I lost my parents. I blamed myself when my parents died. I always thought if I wouldn't have gone to work that day, we would all be happy together. Then the blame shifted to the malicious prosecution that put me there. I hated what they did because if I wouldn't have been in prison, my parents wouldn't have died.

He was crying pretty hard on the concrete floor in front of me. I didn't know what to do or say. I didn't know how to help. A pain that severe doesn't really ever heal. It just lessens over time.

He brought his eyes back up to mine. "I'm sorry for what I've done to you. I hated everyone who stood for God because I blamed Him for stealing my family. But I remember how much

Susan loved Him and I couldn't honor her memory by holding onto hate.

I never really told anyone this but I only went to church for her. I wanted to make her happy. It was like her entire life was only for Him. I only went through the motion of church and being kind to people after the service, but the truth is, I didn't live for Him. It was a front for people to see, including my wife. I felt like he had taken her from me because he knew I loved her more. It made me want to hate Him. At one point I think I really did."

I took a deep breathe and sat down next to him. We both leaned back against the wall. I took my time before I spoke. I was thinking about how unreal it was to be sitting next to a guard. It made me feel equal for the first time in a long time. I wasn't familiar with helping guards because they all seemed to think they were better. To me we were all human, we all needed Christ. I knew I had to say something and I was going to try to direct him toward Christ again.

I looked over into his crying eyes, "You can't blame yourself for what happened. God didn't do that to you either. God loves you and wants happiness for you. A life without Christ as your cornerstone isn't really living at all. It is just going through the motions. God knows where your heart is and he wants eternity with you. Even though you were not there when your family left, God was."

His face ascended as if a thought of joy crossed his mind. I didn't feel like I had said anything dramatic enough to change his life, but he heard something in my voice that I didn't realize I had said. I shifted my shoulders toward him and he was looking up at the ceiling. He started to smile.

"The firefighter said that their death was instant. He said burning is usually a painful way to die but it was like something protected them until it would be fast and painless." He shook his head as he shifted his eyes down to his feet.

"God was there," he said in a soft voice.

I didn't know how to respond because when I thought of God intervening I thought of Him saving lives. In this case, He saved them from pain, and I could tell it meant a lot that his family didn't suffer. I had a thought that kept crossing my mind. *Why didn't God save them?"*

I had many theories to what the answer may be but my best answer was maybe it had to happen. That may have been what it would take to get Sergeant Woods to put God first in his life. In an eternal perspective, his wife and kid could already be saved. He still needed to make that decision and losing them could help him find God. It would be an incredible sacrifice but sometimes God works in mysterious ways.

He had quit crying by this point in our conversation. He stood up and walked over toward the cell door.

"You have helped me more than you will ever know. I needed your help and I am glad you were generous and forgiving enough to give it. I can't tell you how many times I put my gun in my mouth. I wanted to end it. The pain and suffering was too much and I didn't want to go on.

That day I saw the Bible in your hand reminded me of how much my family loved the Lord. It reminded me of losing them and it brought all the pain back to the surface again. Then I became angry and I wanted to destroy you. I wanted any man that had faith to suffer and you showed me that I can't take it away. It is in you, like it was in my wife and I realized I was the one missing it."

I didn't know how to feel. Joy would have fit, but it still felt wrong due to the circumstances. I wanted to feel that I had done something to save his life but the truth was I didn't. God saved him and used me as a vessel. I did nothing but let God put me in the right place at the right time. It was ironic because I felt my life was an example of being at the wrong place at the wrong time, but maybe, with God, there is no such thing.

"Lord, please, I need your forgiveness," he said as he was about to leave the cell.

I stopped him and stood up by him. I did something that in different circumstances could make my life torture. I put my hand on his shoulder. I felt that he needed comfort. I bowed my head, he followed suit and we prayed. I started to speak first.

"Lord, sometimes we question you. We ask why me or why couldn't it be different? I feel you blessed me with the wisdom to see that nothing is outside your will. I know your plan is perfect and I trust that this road leads to a glorious home. I pray for healing and that this man can find you again. He closed his eyes but you were always there right in front of him. We love you Lord, in Jesus's name I pray, Amen."

I knew that Sergeant Woods had something to say. I could feel that he wanted to pray also but was probably scared. I asked him if he would like to pray. He nodded and started to cry again.

"It has been a long time and I don't know what to say. I am so damaged. I feel my soul weeps with me. I pray that you look into my heart and give me what I need. I think I need you God and I don't want to live like this anymore. Please be with me, I need you Father, Amen."

We both looked up at each other. I watched my enemy transform into a friend right before my eyes. I went through a very hard year with constant antagonizing and I was thankful it was over. I felt a weight leave my shoulders knowing that the torment would subside.

Chapter 14

NOTHER COUPLE MONTHS HAD GONE by and I was happy. My class was going well and I loved to preach the gospel at my sermons. I didn't associate with the sergeant very much but there was an unspoken respect for each other. One day I walked into my cell and there was a home-cooked meal under my pillow. It had a note on it that said, "For a few meals missed." It was spaghetti and garlic bread that tasted better than anything I had ever had. I split it with Gabe because he had gone without those meals just as I did.

It was so great. I had already forgiven him for his actions, but the meal was a bonus. Life in that split second of time felt peaceful. I wasn't worried about prison life or people. I was enjoying that moment as if life was a job well done.

The sad part about life was what goes up must come down and it did. A couple months later, a new face came around. His name was Dominick Black. He was Cyrus Black's nephew. He was there for drug trafficking for his uncle's gang operation. Cyrus was still in segregation from killing Jesse. I hoped that his nephew wasn't as hard as he was. The prison had calmed down quite a bit since Cyrus had been gone and I liked the change. I didn't have to look over my shoulder as often but it was still prison.

Dominick was just a kid. He looked a little like his uncle, except he wasn't bald. He had the same facial features though. They both had sharp jaws and were stalky people. I could see the family resemblance. He was young, probably in his early twenties or so. I learned quickly he didn't have the instant aggression that Cyrus had. Cyrus was cold and wicked, but I didn't see that look in his nephew's eyes.

When Dominick got to prison, he was instantly part of the KPK. He had the tough man strut as he walked around the yard—shoulders back, chest out, and chin up was how they all seemed to move. The KPK moved as a pack, mostly for protection. They moved around as if they were the strongest people on earth.

They operated like an army. They were very organized and always had men standing guard in their territory on the ball field. For a group of inmates, they operated very efficiently. I wished that they would put that kind of energy into something more positive, but they were the most closed-minded of everyone there. I thought about them up until my sermon.

I didn't think they were tough. I thought they were lost and weak. I thought they wasted their time destroying everything in their path. I thought that some had good traits but they used them in such wicked ways. My greatest thought was I thought I could help them.

I walked into my cell after my service. That night I talked about the value of integrity. It was a good sermon in my mind and I felt I was getting better with time. I started to think back into my memories. I thought back to day one of the trial. I thought about my supernatural experiences of bliss. I thought about how thankful I was to know there is a God.

I almost found it humorous when people would argue that there wasn't. It was like telling me to believe the sky isn't blue or concrete isn't hard. From what I know in my experiences and from how the English vocabulary defines those terms, I can determine those statements aren't true. As the statement God isn't real would also be false.

There was a point in my Christian life when I went from believing there was a God, to knowing it. Only when I crossed that road was when I realized it was there. A lot of people believe that becoming Christian is the last step and in all reality it is the first. Once I became selfless and thought about what ways I could serve Christ rather than have Christ serve me was when I felt my mind had been truly transformed. I believe that is true Christianity. I realized that was the beginning of my journey and I found total contentment and happiness in God alone.

Gabe walked into the cell as I was lounged on my bunk day-dreaming. My mind raced throughout the day. I would constantly think of new sermons or life lessons. I wanted to help people through tough times. I wanted people to be happy and I shared with them what made me happy. I wanted to spend my life spreading the good news. I felt it was my calling but at the same time I think it is every-one's calling, but way too few follow it.

It was unexplainable how God would draw me to certain peo-ple. I felt like His hand has been guiding me throughout my entire life. In fact, I prayed for that more than any other prayer. I prayed that whatever He wanted me to do, He would make it blatantly obvi-ous. If He laid down the road, I would walk it. So when I felt drawn to do something positive, I felt it was God showing me what to do. I used to always think that I controlled my life, but in all reality, I don't think I had much control at all.

"Where were you at?" I asked Gabe as he walked in.

"I was out and about, living the dream," he replied.

"Did you notice the new kid on the yard?"

"Yes, I did," He said with a nod.

He climbed up onto the desk and then his bunk. He laid down softly as I continued to speak to him.

"I think the kid doesn't fit in with the gang crowd. He seemed to look lost or out of his comfort zone. He seems to be different than the rest. Hopefully, he still has hope."

Gabe dropped his head down on his pillow.

"Yeah, I hope you're right," he said before we both began to doze off.

That night, I had a wonderful dream or more of a memory. I had a memory of back when I was a kid. I was running around the lawn with my dad chasing me through the sprinklers. I had forgotten that it had ever happened. Mom walked out of the front door with a few glasses of ice cold lemonade. I remember how beautiful of a day it was. The sun shined so gloriously throughout the bright blue sky. I remember the laughter we all shared as a family the most. I laughed uncontrollably as we ran over the freshly cut grass.

Mom was smiling a big, beautiful smile with both glasses of lemonade in her hands. After she called at us, we walked up to the front porch. Dad had his hand on my shoulder. I even remembered I was wearing my favorite pair of swimming trunks. They were blue with a picture of a sandy beach on the left leg. I walked up to mom to grab my lemonade. I saw my hand reaching out toward her when suddenly, I woke up to a gun shot.

The siren was blaring and it was loud. It made me panic from not knowing what was going on. I found out later that a couple of inmates had tried to escape in the early morning. They were cooks at the chow hall. Instead of going to work, they tried to sneak over the east side wall. I have no idea how they got outside and around the guards, but it still didn't work out for them. One was shot in the head as he was crawling over the wall with a rope and make-shift grapple. The other surrendered immediately after his friend's lifeless corpse fell to the ground. That's what I heard had happened anyways. We spent the rest of the day on lockdown. The next day, I showed up to my Bible study and one of the men attending my class seemed very off.

"What's wrong?" I asked.

He shook his head at me to imply nothing but I could tell he was lying. I asked if it had to do with what had happened yesterday morning. At that point, the poor man started to cry.

"They shot my cousin."

I sighed because I hated death. I didn't want anyone to lose those they love, especially unexpectedly. It seemed most of the time it would happen that way though. He continued crying, "They shot Juan, man. I grew up with him. Why did he try to leave? He only had four years left to be free."

He started to cry more and blabber out in Spanish that I couldn't thoroughly understand, but I think he said something about celebrating a birthday together. It wasn't very common to open up to each other in prison, especially in a prison like I was in. It was also extremely uncommon to talk to anyone that was not the same race.

It was different in my class though, that behavior was left at the door. Out on the yard, I was just another white man that shouldn't be associated with, but in class we respected each other. I was certain we would have associated with each other if we could but on the yard some things were not acceptable by our peers. I didn't like that it was the way it was, but I couldn't change it.

It felt like I was becoming a magnet to broken people. I think it was more like Christ is close to the brokenhearted and with Christ in me, I could help healing. Every situation was different though. Some men turned angry and others turned sad. I was learning how to help them at whatever point they were at. Regardless, the only thing I could really do was pray and be supportive. God was the one doing all the work.

I did everything I could to help him with the loss of Juan. I knew he cared about his family. Every man I knew in prison cared about someone or something, no matter how ruthless of a person they may be. The most notorious psychopath to hit the yard in twenty years, Cyrus Black, still cared about his brothers in arms.

I talked and tried to comfort him up until we had to leave the chapel. I did everything I could think of to help him. I wanted him to know that God was still by his side and wants a future of hope for him. I prayed for him too because I felt it was the most important part of healing. I knew God had to be part of the process because that was the only way to become truly healed. He embraced it and that helped the entire process.

It is such an experience, seeing someone broken that wants the Lord in their life. They are so passionate and embracing of the truth. I love seeing people search and find the Lord. The moment when they become enlightened is one of the most beautiful parts of life.

I left feeling better because I felt that the seed had been planted. As long as he watered it, he would grow closer and closer to God.

I went home for the rest of the day. When I got there, Gabe was in one of his deep thinking moods. I could always tell when he was in that mood because every time I said something to him, he didn't seem to hear me. He was focused on the thoughts drifting throughout his mind. I knew what it was like because I did the exact same thing.

I traveled into my mind, searching through memories. I loved thinking back to all the times in my life where I was overflowed with joy. I tended to think of my past far more often then I did my future. It was the part of my life that I could see and I loved to remember what shaped me into the man I had become. Good or bad, I still appreciated and embraced my past.

I didn't know what to think of my future. Most people think about retirement or grandkids, but my life had been the same since I was a teenager. It was different living a life in prison. I would be living the same lifestyle as I did when I walked in as to when I become an old man. I was still grateful though because even with the hand I was dealt I could still achieve greatness.

The perspective was what changed the most in me. When I was young, I lived for prestige and luxury. I wanted to be wealthy and well-known. I wanted everyone to see that I had made greatness out of my life. But it changed; it was different. I lived for more than myself. I lived for the Lord and to me that was the greatest choice of lifestyle.

I got Gabe's attention after several frustrating minutes. Once he changed his focus to me, all I wanted to know was what he was thinking so profoundly about.

"What were you thinking about?" I asked him bluntly. He turned to me with a confused look.

"If you could define yourself with one adjective what would you pick?" He asked.

I thought for a second, I had asked myself that question before. If I were to say humble then that answer would contradict itself.

I felt I was humble but that was an adjective for others to give. I didn't know what to pick. Some people might pick their occupation, while others might choose something like loving, caring, or honest. I wanted to pick something that I felt my heart truly felt. I felt I couldn't define myself with one word. I felt I could offer so much more to the world than one defining trait. I still wanted to pick just one for the sake of the question but I couldn't decide. I was battling between joyful, generous, and so many words like them.

"I don't know really, but if I had to pick one I would probably pick honored," I said.

Gabe smiled and said, "Yeah, I could see why you would pick that with the way your life is."

I gave him a quick nod. "What about you? What word did you pick?"

He started to laugh a little. "Why do you think I was thinking so hard? That is a difficult question to answer because there are a bunch of great words to choose from. I'm actually surprised you replied so fast."

"Well, I have one for you," I said.

"Yeah, what is it?"

"Inspirational," I said as I sat down on my bunk.

Chapter 15

I WOKE UP WITH THE thought that I was going to have a great day. The morning went by and I felt happy. Breakfast was fine and nothing out of the ordinary was going on. I enjoyed it. I remember the afternoon too. It was bright and sunny, so I decided to go outside. The sky was so beautiful. It had a few glorious clouds traveling over the horizon and I had the feeling that life was great. I was getting ready to go to the chapel as part of my daily routine when my heart dropped.

I saw the most dreaded face I had ever seen in my entire life. He was outside by the bench press. I stared at the tattoo on his chest. It was the letters KPK. The Ks were both made to look like AK-47s. The magazine and grip formed the K, and the first K was backwards mirroring over to the last. The P in the middle resembled a key. It was tattooed to look like bone and the top was a skull. It was to ensure that everyone knew who held the keys to the KPK.

I despised his look. His face represented evil and his eyes were empty. He had put on quite a bit of muscle during his stay in segregation. I was mostly disgusted that he was out. I couldn't get myself to believe it but I could see him right in front of my eyes. I figured he would be in segregation for life. It had been just over seven years since Jesse was murdered. It instantly brought up the memory of Black brutally taking another man's life, and that man was my friend. He had a no remorse, no sympathy attitude. That man had evil in his soul and I dreaded the thought of him.

The sight of him caused my emotions to peak. I was at the point in my life where I was willing to take a risk. I wasn't afraid and I was sick of all the death and violence on the yard. I wanted to become a virus to the corruption of prison politics. My next goal was to conquer, with the help of God. I felt I could do more to impact the ones that still had hope. I could show everyone the power of Jesus. I wanted to start with the less violent inmates and move my way out like a ripple effect. It was easy to preach to the believers but it is very hard to preach to the unbelievers. They would spit in my face, yell and scream hate, and even try to take my life.

I was okay with the risk. I didn't want to sit the sidelines anymore. I couldn't let Jesse's death be in vain. I tried to make an impact but I wasn't doing enough. I was going to devote the rest of my life to destroy the evil that took his. I had so many emotions arise that I was willing to do anything to fight the evil.

I went to my cell because I wanted to talk to the only man I trusted on the complex. I wanted to ask Gabe what he thought of taking prison politics head on.

"Gabe, I have an idea to run by you and I will need your help."

"What's that?" He replied.

"We both know the impact the church has had on the facility but this place is still awful. I don't want any more hurt or hate. I want to change this place entirely, starting at the core. I want to attack prison politics head on, all the way to the top."

Gabe took several seconds as if he was composing his thoughts.

"Have you prayed about it?" He asked.

I thought he would have answered my question a little more directly. I never knew how Gabe would respond to my ideas but I did know that I would get an honest answer.

"I haven't prayed about it, but I will."

He gave me a simple grin, "I love how on fire you are for the Lord. The most important part of success is passion. Christ had passion for saving all who believe in Him from their sins. He was successful. Remember though, hate can't be taken from this world because it was put here for a purpose. The goal shouldn't be to destroy hate because you can't. It should be to show people that there is an alternative to hate. It is to love.

In order to show that to people, you have to be that light. When a man insults you, repay him with a compliment or when a man strikes you, tell him God loves him. This road will be the hardest road you have ever taken but remember Jesus took that road a long time ago."

I felt at that moment, I may have bitten off more than I could chew. I was a good man but I didn't know if I was capable of being that passive with my prison mentality. I had become more passive as I aged but this situation would be different. I would have to love the man who murdered my friend right in front of my eyes. *How could I love such an extreme evil?"*

"Gabe, how do you keep that mindset so constantly?" I asked. He smiled.

"I have every emotion you do. I feel angry or sad at times, but I always keep in mind the sun is always shining."

"What does that mean?" I asked as I stood up. I leaned toward him and listened a little more intently.

"Well, the sun still shines on a cloudy day. People seem to only notice the clouds but the sun is still shining very beautifully on the earth. It is like the way that God shines on earth. When you gain the ability to realize the sun is always over the clouds, you will become happy regardless of life's turmoil. Day or night, the sun is always shining. Even with the weather constantly changing from bright to stormy, the sun is always shining down. Every day I wake up I do the same thing. I pray and I remember that the sun shines down on the earth, just as the Son shines down on the earth."

I was instantly enlightened at Gabe's words of wisdom. I loved his way with words. I was still afraid but even more, I was determined. It was going to be a battle that I was prepared to fight. I knew once I started down the road I would become a target. My life would be on the line constantly but it already belonged to Christ. In a way, I felt I had nothing to lose.

I sat down on my bunk and grabbed my Bible. I started to pray. "Lord, I know that you have been by my side. I'm asking for your help. I need your protection, perseverance, and wisdom to be part of me. I'm ready to fight the good fight. I love you and will devote everything to you. In Jesus's name I pray, Amen."

I slept very soundly that night. I woke up and walked to breakfast with Gabe. Sergeant Woods was still working on our tier. He had been a blessing in my life ever since he had found God again. He was dating a woman on the outs that was in the church band. He would talk to me every now and then, but it wasn't very consistently. He told me how coming to Christ sincerely this time had changed his life. He was proud of the man God made him. I was happy for him too.

Gabe and I had made the plan of bringing Christ to the population rather than letting them come to us. We decided to start with the less violent of the inmates to get some practice. We both knew that for every attempt of bringing a man to Christ, we would have ten failures. Most people there didn't want to hear the news. They wanted to only be accountable to themselves. It was hard to accept that some were too lost to be found, but it wasn't going to stop me from trying to save the others who were still searching.

I wanted to start with a seminar and invite as many people as I could. I put in the paperwork to the warden and explained what it would be. With my reputation, he accepted. I felt like the first steps were taken and we would only gain momentum from there on. I had made a lot of contacts in the Christian society, so I was going to tap into that resource. I called a pastor that had preached for us before and asked if he could get a band to play. That was all allowed and I was ecstatic.

It was called the "What's your Number?" seminar and it was based upon integrity. I wanted people to think about holding themselves accountable rather than guards or other authority. The principle it was built on was if there was a table with a substantial amount of money on it, at what point would you take the money? The money was not yours and you knew it was stealing. Also, you would never get caught. The question was, when or if you would sell your integrity? Would you sell it for a hundred, thousand, million, or more? Would you sell it at all? What's your number?

I had flyers made to hand out at the chapel. A lot of people laughed about it and it found its way to a trash can frequently. We had live music coming from the outside and a guest speaker. I did as much ground work as I could. I would have packed the entire prison population into the chapel if they would all be saved. When the date came around, more people attended than I thought would. It still wasn't packed full but a few new faces showed up. I don't think very many at all were part of the gang scene but it still made an impact on other inmates.

The music was amazing. They were a very talented band. The sermon was awesome with several points on integrity being related to scripture. At the end of the seminar, we had people write on a piece of paper what they thought their number was. People had a lot of fun writing several zeros and nines on their paper. At that point the pastor got serious.

A man had written a million dollars on his paper. The pastor asked him if it was just one dollar less, would he still take the money.

He replied back to the pastor, "For a dollar, it's just a dollar. I would still take the money." He dropped the amount suddenly.

"What about for fifty grand?" The pastor asked.

"No way, I would want more," the man replied.

"But you would be set for life with commissary. You would have nothing but the best food you could get. Everything would be paid for," the pastor said. He mentioned several more reasons and the man eventually folded.

"Okay, I would take the money," the man said.

He kept bringing the man's number down more and more, little by little, until he asked the man if he would take it if it was a single dollar.

"No way, not for a dollar. It isn't worth it, not a chance," the man said.

"But it's only a dollar," the pastor replied. He waited a few seconds and walked off the stage toward the other man speaking.

"No one would ever miss it and people sell their integrity for an extra dinner tray all the time. Who would miss it? You said it yourself, it's just a dollar."

The man was in shock. He looked down at his shoes in shame.

"Honestly, I would probably take the dollar," he said hesitantly.

Several other men in the crowd showed his same emotion. It was a wake up call to some inmates. They didn't realize how often they sold their integrity. It wasn't designed to make them feel bad but to show them what they were too callous to see. Some people shared that they would steal paper or indigent soap, which was worth only pennies. He closed the service and talked about Jesus. He was offered food when He was starving and tired in the desert. He was promised the entire world. He was tempted and even when He was weak He still wouldn't take it.

He had a lot of men thinking. So many men put a high price on their integrity but then sold it for very little. It didn't have to be for money. They could sell it by violating any of God's laws. The goal is to be like Christ. He went on preaching for a few more minutes. He talked about ways of keeping our integrity, like being honest and upright. He also talked about how valuable it is and it should be kept sacred. At the end of the seminar, he prayed and then had the room say in unison, "My integrity is not for sale."

Chapter 16

EVERYTHING SEEMED TO BE FOLLOWING the plan. We knew it was going to take time to change people, maybe even a lifetime, but we had a good start going. The next week, I noticed the slightest of changes in a few men around the yard. Mostly in the ones who took the seminar to heart. It did what it was designed to do and that was to get them thinking. At least they were aware of what integrity was. I still knew if it wasn't constant, they would fail. It was that way for me too. I think that is why the Bible says it's a daily battle.

I wanted to speed up the process and change everything instantly, but it didn't work that way. The yard was still run by Black and the KPK. When Cyrus got back from segregation, Dominick was under his authority. Every time I saw the crew together, I saw the way that Cyrus treated everybody. He wasn't afraid to lay hands on anyone, even his own nephew. Dominick was family and was raised around the lifestyle, but he looked out of place. He was different than they were. When I looked at his face, he looked like a lost child. I felt he still had a chance to be saved. I made it a side goal of mine to show him Christ and let God take it from there.

Gabe and I brainstormed constantly throughout the day. We were passionate about showing everyone around us to Christ. We went through the ideas of guest speakers and bands, but it only attracted the same people. They were all interested in the first place. I wanted to spark interest in the ones who didn't have any. It seemed like the only way to get people interested was by showing them, not telling. The problem with that was it took so long. I wanted a large number of people to learn the good news and I felt I could only help one at a time. It was like trying to fill the ocean drip by drip.

I met Gabe out on the ball field. The weather was beautiful outside and I wanted to get some sun. We sat in the east corner away from all the other inmates and talked. Cyrus was out on the ball field too. The KPK had their own section that was only for them. They were not doing much at the time besides looking around. A few members were also doing push-ups but that was it.

"Where do we go from here?" I asked Gabe as we sat down to enjoy the sun.

He was thinking. He put his hands behind his head and leaned back to look up at the sky.

"I think it is time that we shoot for the moon and try to take them from the top."

"You mean try to change Cyrus?" I said a little hesitantly.

"No, not change, but show him and the rest God's love."

We thought quietly for the remainder of the hour. I thought about several topics crossing my mind. I wanted to take a moment to relax about the stress though. I noticed a common bird several yards away from me flying toward the sun. I loved nature, no matter how small. I returned back to my conversation with Gabe once they called recall.

"Well, where do we start?" I asked as Gabe and I stood up.

"We'll start with his nephew," he said dramatically as we were heading home.

I thought about ways to approach Dom the rest of that night. The next day, I went to the chapel and got a copy of the New Testament. It was a palm-sized copy that had been donated to the prison. We had several so I took a copy and looked for Dom out on the ball field. He wasn't directly by the rest of his gang and that was very rare. I took advantage of the opportunity and approached him. I walked up and handed the Bible to him. He looked at me curiously and didn't say anything at first. He read the cover that had New Testament written on the front. He looked back at me and politely said, "Thank you." I thought he would have thrown it at the ground or something to that nature, but he didn't.

That moment taught me a new lesson. It was hard to show the violent people Christ because the reaction was unpredictable. I never knew how they would respond or what they would do. I would constantly hesitate to approach them because I dreaded the insults. Sometimes, God gave me the courage to overcome that fear and most of the time they actually wanted to hear of God's glory. I thought deep down and my honest opinion was I judged those people. I thought that the worst people wouldn't want to hear it but in all reality, they needed it the most.

I got excited from how it went with Dom. I went back to the chapel to get more Bibles to hand out around the prison. I thought that more people might want one. I walked up to a large man that was in for murder. He didn't seem like he was too violent to be approached. I walked up, just as I did with Dom. I reached out and handed him the copy of the Bible. He looked at it and read the cover. I thought to myself, *Another one down, glory to God.* He suddenly dropped the book and in one swift motion smashed his fist into my face.

I wasn't expecting it at all. I fell back onto my rear as blood started to rush down the front of my face. He was a big guy with a strong punch, but I still remained conscious. After he hit me, he didn't continue to swing, but smiled at me and walked away. I sat there with a bloody nose, fat lip, and that small copy of the New Testament right by my side.

I almost found that moment humorous. I couldn't help but smile. It was a realization that I needed to remember where I was. That guy didn't hesitate for a second and others wouldn't either. I sat there for awhile and tilted my head to the sky to stop the bleeding. I started to chuckle. I stood up and saw Gabe walking toward me.

"You okay?" He asked as he walked up.

"Yeah, I'm fine," I said as I wiped the dirt off my pants.

"For a big guy he doesn't hit too hard," I said with a sarcastic smile. Gabe started to laugh at me.

"It's probably because you're so used to it by now," he said. I sighed a little.

"I don't think anyone gets used to it but it becomes less painful," I replied.

I used the bottom of my shirt to clean up the blood so the guards wouldn't notice.

I could feel that we were going to have meaningful conversation again. It seemed like every time something happened in life he had a sliver of wisdom to add to it. We started walking the track surrounding the field and talked.

"Gabe, after all these years, I keep asking myself why God put me here. I have so many questions I want to ask Him. I want to know why He allowed my life to be stolen." Gabe looked up to the bright blue sky. I noticed that most of the time when I asked him questions he would do that. I don't know if it was because he was praying or what, but he was always looking up.

"Luke, how do you make a sword?" He asked.

"What do you mean?" I replied.

"A sword, like what you would take into battle," he responded. I was confused by his question but I went along with it.

"Well, I think you take the metal and cut and shape it until it is sharp," I said.

He smiled at me.

"If you want to make a sword, you put it under extreme heat and then you pound it with a hammer over and over. You shape it with every blow until it takes its correct shape. This makes that sword durable and reliable for when it is taken to battle."

"Yeah, I get it," I responded.

Then he looked at me and said, "What's so different from life's trials. For you, this prison is that furnace and the constant pounding is shaping you. If you ask me why God put this in your life, it's because He wanted you to be refined and strengthened. He wanted you to be prepared and reliable for His battle."

A sudden flash of heat went up my spine. Gabe was so wise. I loved the way he spoke. I still believed that there was more to what happened in my life than only me but I agreed with what Gabe had to say. I think God did want to refine me, but he also wanted to harvest a lot of fruit from this tree. I couldn't help the people in prison if I wasn't around them. I had to endure the pain so I could understand it. I had to know what others experienced so I could relate.

I began to think of how relatable a lot of life's trials were but also so unique. I knew about a different type of pain than a cancer survivor, war vet, or widow, but we all knew what pain felt like. We all understood how gut-wrenching pain could be and some of us understood how to conquer pain. For me, I needed God.

Gabe used such an awesome metaphor. I could see how it related so well. Prison as an innocent man was my furnace and everyone has their own. The best part about it though was God can save anyone from the heat of the fire. It all comes down to trusting His judgment and letting Him lead the way. The Bible does say the Lord is my shepherd for a reason. It's because He knows the best path for shaping us all for the future and to help us have lives worth living.

After our walk and conversation, we spent most of the remainder of our day in our cell. It was unusually quiet for some reason. People were still out and about walking the tier, but the whole area stayed quiet. I took a pleasant nap up until dinner, and then Gabe and I went to church that night.

The next day, I woke up with a dull pain throughout my shoulders. I was a lot older than when I first walked in. My body couldn't take a punch the way it used to. I still smiled as I remembered the look on that man's face after he hit me. His crooked smile made my day.

I knew he thought that he was tough but the truth was he probably hurt others because he feels hurt himself. I had been there and could recognize how he felt. One thing he probably hadn't yet realized was there is a big difference between kindness and weakness. Weakness is running away because you're scared, kindness is walking away because you're not.

I observed a lot of people and watched how they acted on the yard. Most people still walked around with a strut and puffed out chest, but I was more intimidated by the ones who didn't act that way. The scariest type of inmate wasn't the loud ones, but the quiet ones that would react rather than yell. They thought differently than most. I agreed with them, I would rather be tough and people think I'm not, than for people to think I'm tough and not be.

I spent the next week in routine with church and biblical conversation. It was an everyday lifestyle, for me to love the Lord. I wanted to help others and change this place for the better, but I wanted to do it simply because I loved God. In everything I did, I wanted Him to be by me, guiding me through the tough times and worshiping Him through the best times. It was a relationship I valued very much.

I was walking out on the ball field when the kid approached me. Dom walked up.

"I read the book," he said with a slight trace of excitement.

"Great job, now what's next?" I replied with a smile.

His mood changed dramatically. He started to look around scared, like something was going on. I felt a feeling in my stomach as soon as he started to act anxious.

"The gang doesn't allow outside religion. It's all in or I am out. Cyrus has no tolerance after a man tried to step out before I got here. It was great to get some hope but we have to part ways. I have always had a lot of questions but it's not worth my life."

I nodded in agreement, not because he was right but because I didn't want to see the kid hurt. The truth was, it is worth his physical life because his eternal life is far more valuable. I wanted him to receive God's grace. I had that feeling that he wanted to be part of Christ's family more than he wanted to be part of Cyrus's. I could only pray for him and go from there.

Jesus, be with that boy. Help him through this, I said in my head.

I was starting to turn and walk away when Dom turned around.

"Wait!" He said. I looked back at him and waited for him to speak.

"I changed my mind. I have some questions and I think I should get more information before I make a decision. Can we meet up and talk?"

"Yeah, that sounds fine. How about in an hour we meet at the chapel? Most people won't be there at this time."

He nodded his head at me, "See you there."

I spent the remainder of my time out on the ball field looking out at the sky. It was one of my favorite things to do. I loved to lie down and stare at the clouds, even though I wasn't supposed to. We were only allowed to sit but I got away with relaxing on my back from time to time. They had that rule because they had to be able to tell that we were alive by looking at us. I got in trouble for it from time to time but I loved it so much I did it anyway.

Chapter 17

I MADE MY WAY OVER to the chapel. Dom was there and we met as privately as we could in the sanctuary.

"So, what questions did you want to ask?" I said. Dom was listening intently from the beginning and got strait to the point.

"How do you give control of your life to a being that you don't know truly exists?" I smiled at him once he asked. My first thought was, *That's a good question.* I thought for a second at how Gabe would respond because he seemed to be better at those types of questions, but at the same time I knew that question was meant for me.

"That question has been asked by people for centuries. I have asked that same question at times in my life. I'll start by saying the more you search, the more you find. When I was an early Christian, I learned it starts with faith. God started to reveal Himself the more time went on. For me, I have no question if there is a God. I know it to be true. I see it in the small things, like a baby smiling or tears of joy. Faith isn't about certainty. It's about taking the first step without seeing the rest of the staircase."

"Yeah, I understand that, but I guess I feel like I have to be logical. I want God to be proven to me. I want it to be real as everything around me. I don't want to have any questions about who I give my life to," he responded.

"Dom, that is great. I understand how you feel and so many people feel the same way you do. They want clean cut answers and rightly so, but remember, God is the creator not us. He isn't our servant and He shouldn't have to be submissive to our wants. You're asking me to tell you why God hasn't shown Himself to you in an immaculate way, and until He does so then you won't believe in Him. My honest opinion is that that is an arrogant line of thinking. It is like you're saying we are so important God has to prove Himself to us. He doesn't. God is God, and if anything we should have to prove ourselves to Him. Showing faith is a good start."

Dom nodded his head, "Huh, I've never really thought that deeply about it before."

"Dom, I am only trying to help you. But sometimes in life, the best answer is to help yourself. You need answers, but my question for you is how do you find answers?"

Dom looked at me with a puzzled face.

"You search, Dom. You have to look for the answers. The Bible promises that you will find what you're searching for." He nodded and looked down. I could see a little disappointment on his face.

"I wonder if something is wrong with me," he said.

"Why do you feel like that?" I responded.

"I guess it just seems like I have more trouble than everyone around me in accepting God. I can feel that I am not strong enough to take on life by myself but that's why I'm searching in the first place. I feel depressed, like I can't think. I just want to understand and be happy."

I smiled at Dom, "Someone is finding the first steps of Christianity. Having the ability to understand we can't do it on our own is a big step. We need God and choosing to have God lift the burden of our troubles is a better life to live.

Dom, I want to share a little about myself to try to help you relate. I remember a point in my life where I felt very empty inside. I had a void in my being. I felt it physically in the center of my chest but so much more, I felt it spiritually. I was completely unsatisfied in what life had to offer. The ironic part is I was at the highest point in my life, from a worldly perspective anyway.

I had money and freedom. Life was really good from that point of view but inside I was lost. I knew life had more to offer than nice things. After I went to prison, I went through a dark time but God brought me back to the light. He was faithful. My point is, when I had the least in life, I actually had the most. I was fulfilled by the glory of God.

God has always pulled me through every trial. I hear God's voice but only because I have learned to listen. I am trying to tell you that God wants a relationship with you. He wants to listen to your prayers and know that you love Him.

Dom had listened intently to what I had to say. After he left, I didn't know how much he actually took in. I did the best I could to at least plant the seed. All I did know was I wanted to help the men around me. I wanted to make changes for the better and I was going to put all I had into accomplishing those goals.

I wanted earth to be a better place so bad that it hurt. I wanted to help people learn to love. It was a goal that was a little farfetched because the loveliest people didn't usually walk through the prison door. It was mostly gang bangers or addicts, but I still wanted to try. Everyone deserves an opportunity to better their life.

Everything progressed really slowly though. Time went by because of routine but even with me reaching out to the kid and having guest speakers, the place changed very little. I was beginning to get very discouraged. I felt that no matter how hard I tried, it wasn't going to be enough. I loved scripture because when I did feel depressed, I knew what to do. Jesus says to draw near. That's what I did. I spent my day reading God's word and praying. I prayed for everything I could think of. I prayed for hungry kids on the streets, for widows and orphans, and for the people that didn't know Christ, for them to seek Him.

About a month after I was feeling that way, I was walking to the chapel for my weekly Bible study. I walked around the corner of the hallway that led to the laundry room. I came around the corner and saw two men beating up a younger guy. I didn't hesitate for a second because the guy looked really beat up. I dropped my stuff, ran, and slammed into the guy on top. His buddy started swinging at me and my fight mode turned on. I ducked his left hook and hit him in the stomach.

His buddy was just getting up out of the corner of my eye. I swung my right arm and backhanded him in the temple. He dropped straight to the ground. The other one had recovered from the stomach shot and I kicked the inside of his right knee. I heard a snap and a little yelp as he fell down grasping his leg.

They were both down so I moved over to the kid that they jumped. He must have been just over eighteen years old at the most. He was in really bad shape. His left side of his face was completely swollen. His jaw was slightly turned in and he was spitting blood as he struggled to breathe. The sound he made as he struggled to breathe was awful. I felt helpless. I knew if I wouldn't have stepped in they would have killed him.

I thought about lifting him up and bringing him to a guard. If he didn't get medical attention quick, he could still die. His tongue looked like it was cut from his teeth being smashed in. I prayed for the young kid and I didn't want him to die so early in life. It didn't matter to me why he was prison, I just wanted to help him. He was lying on the concrete, falling in and out of consciousness. Seconds went by but they felt like hours.

I had my head on a swivel as I was taking a few seconds to decide what to do. The other man got up and limped over to his unconscious friend. The guy woke up but he was still dazed. He pulled him up on his shoulder. I was standing there in a fighting stance in case they tried to attack me. I got an evil glare as they limped off.

I turned back at the kid. His body was starting to go into shock. I took off running toward my unit. I had no idea why a guard wasn't closer by. As I started to run, I looked up and saw that the camera that faced into that part of the laundry was turned away from the scene.

I ran into J-block, which was about fifty yards away, and spotted Sergeant Woods. He was up at the front desk reading some paperwork. He looked up at me and I yelled at him, "Come quick, it's an emergency." He could tell by the tone in my voice that I wasn't joking. He jumped up said something into his radio as he ran out with me. A couple other guards hustled out of the watch bubble and went with us.

I brought him straight to the kid. I didn't want to move the body incase he had a neck injury. Sergeant Woods called a lockdown on the radio and sent for a medical team. He told me to go back to the cell as two other guards arrived at the scene. I listened and turned back to my unit as a guard escorted me home.

After about an hour or two, the sergeant walked up to my cell. I was sitting on my bed worried for the kid. Gabe and I prayed constantly for his well-being. Sergeant Woods opened my door and walked in.

"Luke, what happened?" I began to stand up and he put his hand up to tell me to stay seated.

"I was headed to the chapel when I saw that kid getting assaulted by two guys. I smashed into one and knocked him out. The other I hit his knee and punched him in the gut. I was protecting the kid."

The sergeant nodded his head as he was listening, "I believe you but we have to initiate an investigation. The kid is in a coma and we don't have a camera view to see what happened. I'm going to have to put you in segregation until it gets all sorted out. It is procedure, you know that."

I thought to myself, *I've heard that one before*. Regardless, I calmly nodded my head and turned around. Sergeant Woods put hand cuffs on my wrists. It almost felt like the first time. It had been a long time since I had felt the cool steel squeeze against my skin and I didn't miss it. I did what I did for all the right reasons and I felt as if I was going to get punished for it. To me that was one of the most discouraging parts of incarceration but this time it was different. I trusted Sergeant Woods was on my side and would vouch for me. I spent a couple days in the hole before Sergeant Woods came in.

"I have some good news," he said as he walked in.

"We had another camera that had a partial view of the incident. I saw some of what happened and could put the whole picture together. Nice punch by the way," he said with his unique smirk.

"The kid is okay and he'll have a full recovery. He doesn't remember a whole lot but he won't have any long-term damage. If you wouldn't have stepped in, he would be having a funeral rather than a recovery." I was glad the kid would be okay.

"Good deal." I said. Sergeant Woods looked back at me.

"His name is Matthew by the way and he's a police officer's son. I think that's why he was targeted but we're still looking into it. For now the assailants are being moved to segregation. You did a good thing, Luke."

I nodded and said, "Thank you."

I was curious what the son of a police officer could have done to go to prison, most of the time I thought of an officer's son as being a law-abiding citizen. I knew the system well enough to understand some crazy events can happen but a police officer's son usually didn't fit the stereotype of the people who became inmates.

"What's he in prison for in the first place?" I asked.

He smiled at me and gave me a unique look, "You know I'm not supposed to talk about peoples' crimes. It wouldn't be ethical for me to share that information with just anyone. But I know I can trust you. He's in for involuntary manslaughter. From everything I read in his paperwork, it looked like he made a terrible mistake. He was drinking on his prom night and rolled his truck. His date was ejected and killed at the scene. All around it was a tragedy."

I shook my head when I spoke, "I hate the law sometimes. In some cases, it is really hard to get justice. It was horrible that the young girl was killed and nothing can bring her back. But most of all, I hate the situation as a whole. Hopefully, he will learn from his actions and understand the effects of drinking and driving. I wish I had an answer that would help everyone."

I had a sinking feeling hit my stomach. It really bothered me that in the system destroying another life makes up for the one lost. It's an eye for an eye to the fullest. I wanted to find both parties involved and preach forgiveness. I consistently had the mindset of helping.

"What they don't know is prison could make him a worse person. The years of negative could easily change his mindset. He could get caught up in the wrong crowd. One life has already been lost. Why take another? I really hope that the other family seeks Christ and forgives. That is such a horrible situation to be in but holding on to blame will only haunt everyone involved."

Sergeant Woods nodded in agreement. He didn't have much to add to what I said. They let me out of The Hole and I instantly got back into my routine. I spent the next couple weeks waiting for the kid to recover. I kept in contact with Sergeant Woods by asking him how Matthew was doing. He had a broken jaw and took a severe beating so they kept him in the infirmary for a while. I was sickened by how ruthless people were.

They would have killed a young kid because his dad enforced the law. I didn't know if I believed that was the real reason why he was attacked. It could be true or they could have had no reason at all. Prison was a scary place where crazy things happened. Logically, people believe that they must have had a reason, but they could have done it for something as minimal as a power trip. All I knew was I was disgusted at the constant gruesome attacks. They happened nearly every day.

I kept replaying the attack in my head. What I saw disturbed me. The man was holding the young, unconscious boy by the front of his shirt and kept swinging as hard as he could. He smashed his fist into him over and over again. At least the kid was unconscious most of the attack.

It made me so angry that they attacked the weak like they did. I was glad I was there to help because most inmates would have kept walking like nothing happened. Eventually, someone would walk up on his corpse and the prison couldn't do anything but an investigation after that. I prayed for the boy consistently. I wanted him to have a swift and full recovery.

I felt like I had very little control. All I could do was pray. I wanted so badly to go put healing hands on him and watch him recover instantly. All the violence was such a common part of my life in prison, but it never got any easier to accept. I wouldn't accept that it was right to live like that. I wanted love and I wanted encouragement to be shared, rather than hate and punishment. I felt the harder I tried to help, the harder it got.

I knew it was Satan trying to discourage me. I did what the Lord says to do when I felt that way. I focused on Christ. I prayed for that kid to recover daily until one day he did. Months had gone by since the attack and the kid was back on the yard. One part of me felt sad because he was back and I didn't want him to go through anything like that ever again, but the other was happy because I had proof he was alive and well.

He would always have a constant reminder of what happened to him. He had a scar run across his jaw where the surgical team did reconstructive surgery. It started just under his earlobe and went to the bottom of his chin. Once I saw him, I approached him without thought. I wanted to see how he felt. I walked up to him.

"How are you doing?" I asked. He looked at me a little confused as if he didn't know who I was. I had forgotten he was unconscious by the time I had got there so he wouldn't know who I was.

"I'm okay," he said a little hesitantly back at me.

"I'm Luke. I was the one who stopped the attack and got the guards." His eyes lit up with joy.

"You were the one who saved me?" He asked.

I nodded my head, "Yeah, I guess you could say it like that."

"O gosh, thank you so much," he said with a look of joy. His eyes started to tear up. "I don't know what else to really say," he added.

"Well, you're welcome," I said grinning. He smiled back slightly.

"I don't really know what happened. I was walking back to my cell and they attacked me out of nowhere. I was so scared and didn't know what to do. They were so strong and I remember getting pinned and hit. The next thing I knew I was waking up in the hospital. I didn't know what happened but Sergeant Woods told me that another inmate had stopped the attack. I didn't know who it was but now I know it was you. I'm glad to finally have been able to meet you. Thank you again for saving me."

"Well, I'm glad you're recovering." I said. He walked away and smiled as if his life was a gift.

I felt honored to be someone's hero. I believe we all have a hero. He saved more than our lives, He saved our souls. He freed us when we were beaten and pinned from the power of sin. He gave up everything for us and all He asks in return was for us to love and accept Him. All we have to do is simply accept our king, our everlasting king.

Chapter 18

I BEGAN TO DEVELOP A relationship with Matthew. Matthew was driven and ambitious. I liked that in a someone's personality. He started volunteering at the church and was the type of person I wanted to be around. I was excited for him because I loved to see the Holy Spirit work in people. He realized that his life was not his own and he wanted to dedicate it to the Lord. It made me feel like a proud father, even though I never had the privilege of being a dad at that time.

We began having great biblical conversations together. I loved group fellowship in the church but a close one-on-one conversation about the glory of God is priceless. Nothing has made me feel so joyful in all my life. I loved the lifestyle. I had to renew myself daily and was always looking for the opportunity to do God's work.

Matthew wanted to learn of God's glory. It reminded me of my young years of being on fire for the Lord. I wanted to show him everything I could and prayed that he would have the wisdom to take it all in. I prayed that God would work through me. I wanted Matthew's relationship to remain clear. I wanted nothing to be in between him and the altar. In a way, I wanted to give him everything I wanted for myself.

I remember the majority of our conversations. One took place in the early morning. We had already had breakfast and the guards had barely opened the ball field for the inmate population. I had made arrangements to meet Matthew out on the dirt track surrounding the field. He was out there already when I showed up. We started to pace the track and enjoy the conversation.

I enjoyed taking in every view. I watched people and stared at the sky. I couldn't see very far out in the distance because the wall blocked my view. But I could see the giant concrete tower that stood in the corner of the prison. A guard was always standing with his rifle looking down at us. He would pace back and forth while the guard next to him stared at us through his binoculars.

I always wondered how much better my life could be if I entered as a guard rather than an inmate. I wanted to be able to talk to them to ensure they didn't take their freedom for granted. But freedom, like most things, isn't valued until it is gone.

I daydreamed a lot. It didn't matter where I was in the prison; my mind was always racing. It was constantly concentrated on influencing everyone around me for the better.

Everything was normal that day besides the conversation between Matthew and me. I had finally told him my life story. I told him about the trial and conviction. I told him about my parents and the struggles I had through my stay in prison. I told him that I forgave the people who did this to me but when he questioned the statement I did too.

"Do you really forgive them? They stole your life away from you for no reason. How could you forgive someone for that?" He asked.

I stood there shocked by the blatant questioning. I had gone all these years thinking I had forgiven them. I prayed for forgiveness and even preached it to others. But I knew I still held on to some resentment. I always tried to cover it up because I didn't want them to have any power over me.

I remembered from time to time how I wanted them to feel some of the hurt. I wanted them to know what it felt like to be shattered by the lies and destruction of their doing. I wanted vengeance but I knew that the Bible says, *Vengeance is for the Lord.* As a Christian, I should want to forgive them because Christ has forgiven me, but it was a more difficult task than I thought.

I had swells of emotion flourish over me. For a second I even felt hate. It had been so long since I had felt that. I thought I would never feel that way again. But it was still there locked deep down in a closet of emotion that I had packed full. I knew my soul truly didn't hate them and with time, I would heal and forgive. I simply struggled because of the amount of pain I had. At that moment, I fell victim to Satan's temptation.

I was disappointed in myself. I thought that part of my life was gone. I was wrong. It shows that when we believe we are untouchable, we learn that we are most vulnerable. I knew it was something I needed to address soon because living life with hate was not the type of life God intended for us.

I prayed for myself. I wanted healing once and for all. I wanted it all behind me so that for the remainder of my life, I would feel love for the people that wronged me. That is a gift only God can give.

Scripture says, "Even the pagans will love each other." It's easy to love those who are good to you, but try loving those who shame and lie about you. It is a very difficult task. It is important to love the unlovable. It says to pray for those who have wronged you. I tried that and thought I had succeeded, but deep down I didn't truly feel that way. I felt hurt and discouraged. I had only gone through the motions of forgiveness. If I would have truly forgiven, then my heart would wish to have my enemies succeed. It's hard to comprehend but the feeling of wishing your enemies to prosper takes the purest type of love. It takes God, so I prayed for them to be blessed. I wanted to truly feel it too because I couldn't lie to myself anymore. I had to finally let go.

I snapped back to reality and continued my conversation with Matthew. We debated and the conversation ended well. I realized I needed healing. I replayed the memories in my head about the trial. I questioned why God would put me through it. I thought of people in the Bible, like Joseph, who also went to prison for a crime he never committed. I became sad because I felt that the world was packed with injustice. It hurt me to think like that so I followed the Bible's instruction.

I spent the rest of the day in prayer and reading. I had read the Bible front to back more times than I knew. I still picked up something different from it every time I studied. As I grew in my Christian maturity, my perception of God's word grew with me.

The same scripture I had read in my youth would sometimes be interpreted differently as I grew older. It makes it so much more beautiful. It is like seeing something in a painting I never noticed before. I could have looked at the same beautiful piece of art every day for my entire life but when the light shines on it from a slightly different angle, then I could see something there I had never noticed before.

It's beautiful how objective parts of life can be. Everything can change based upon mood or circumstances. It shows how complex God can be and also so simple. He can simply respond to a question or sometimes he will wait for us to be ready before he gives the answer. The greatest enigma is how his timing is always flawless, but our perception determines whether we believe that to be true or not.

God's word is perfect and constant, but that doesn't mean we are. When we change, so will our perceptions. I prayed over and over that the slight resentment that I held on to would subside. It moved like the waves of an ocean. I felt it at times and at others it drifted back to sea.

A few days later, I continued my conversation with Matthew. I brought it up casually. It was unique for me because most of the in-depth conversations I had were with Gabe. I enjoyed the conversations with Matthew though because he was so young. He had a gentle spirit and innocence about him that was inspiring.

"I have been thinking a lot about forgiveness," I said. He turned to me and replied, "Yeah, what about it?"

"Well, I realized that I was wrong. I have always told myself that I had forgiven them because that is what the Bible says to do. I did it because I was told to rather than because I wanted to."

Matthew listened intently as I spoke. His look was so pure and soft. I realized how much the kid had humbled me without knowing it. It was ironic because I saved Matthew's life and yet, I felt indebted to him. It was amazing how well God had worked through him because I needed humbling and I never realized it.

"I prayed for the people who persecuted me and the more I prayed for my pain to be lifted, the better I felt. I could feel the pressure lifting, little by little, and I truly believe the more I pray, the more it becomes sincere.

It was very hard to ask for those who persecuted me to be blessed but through God I believe I really want it. The worldly side of me felt like I wanted revenge but the true me knew I had to let go. All I know now is the whole me wants them to be blessed and forgiven."

My emotions were peaking at that moment. I couldn't help but to let some of them out and I started to cry. It was weird to have a moment of vulnerability but it felt right. I almost found it funny. There I was, a seasoned inmate, and he was a young, new kid, but I opened up anyways. I trusted that God had put him in my life for a reason. I felt my chains of confinement being broken as I broke down and cried. That was the moment when the burden I had against my enemies slipped away and I never felt it again.

Matthew did nothing more than be at the right place at the right time. Sometimes that is all God wants us to do. The Lord does so much good work without us realizing it. I believe he has more control than we know. Sometimes people feel he is distant but he is constantly close. He is watching and loving, we just have to take time to notice.

I have heard of people becoming angry at God when something petty happens, like their car won't start. The truth is that could be God protecting them. He may have protected them from being at the wrong intersection at the wrong time and saved their life.

People don't know what he saves us from because they don't experience what could have been. It makes me feel nothing but gratitude. It makes me think of scripture and to not lean onto my own understanding. My mindset is to trust Him because God promises He will be there always and forever.

Chapter 19

I WAS PREACHING AT THE chapel when a familiar face walked in. Dominick was still part of the KPK, so I didn't associate with him much. I tried to do what I could and was still trying to destroy prison politics, but I was only one man. We had several guest speakers and bands, but it was still a struggle to create any change. I didn't know how to bring Christ to the ones who rejected Him. I handed out Bibles but it seemed like no one would listen.

I was chased away several times. My life has been threatened and I had more than enough run-ins with trouble. I was trying my best to spread the gospel but the people in prison didn't usually care to listen. I had to do my best with the hand I was dealt, so my only choice was to be persistent.

Dom came in and sat at the back. I hadn't started my sermon yet. He kept his head down and was trying not to draw attention. Nobody paid him any more than a glance except me. I tried not to draw any attention to him either but I was happy to see he made it to church. I wanted to go up and speak to him, but my wisdom told me that it would be better to keep him under the radar.

I preached that night about the gift of free will. I saw Dom was paying attention to God's message. I was glad that he was too. I changed what my message was going to be strictly for him. I wanted him to know that he had the choice to choose God. He could be part of Christ's family and all he had to do was accept Christ as his Lord and Savior. He needed to accept the truth because it is only through Christ that we are saved.

The next day, I saw Dom out on the ball field. He was next to Cyrus by the bench press. The KPK kept that as their territory. I noticed the left side of Dom's face was black and blue with bruises. I didn't know what had happened to him but I doubt it was a coincidence that Cyrus's right hand was bruised at the knuckles. He must have hit him and that type of beating wasn't from only one punch. He was punishing him probably for disobeying an order. Maybe the order was to stay away from the church but I don't know.

It disgusted me that a man was trying to change for the better and kept getting pulled down. I wanted nothing more than for him to be part of the family of God but I felt helpless. What could I do? I couldn't force him to make the decision and I wouldn't want to anyways. I could take Cyrus out of the picture but not by Christian means. My hands were tied and it was very frustrating.

I knew if he didn't have the negative influences in his life, he could make better decisions. I was in a standstill because my best option was to be patient but I felt that it had to change soon otherwise we would lose him.

I became discouraged. I went home and met up with Gabe in our cell. I was angry because of my frustration. The kid was clearly reaching out but I couldn't hold him above water. I was upset and sometimes I let Gabe know.

I yelled at Gabe, "Why doesn't God do something?" He put down his book and gave me his full attention.

"Why does he let people live like this?" I said.

Gabe sat up and hung his feet off his bunk. I started to blabber on about my frustrations as Gabe calmly listened. I had so many wants and they were good and unselfish wants too. They were all what I thought God would have wanted so I was confused why God wouldn't grant them. I ranted on for several minutes about everything crossing my mind.

He was a great listener and as usual, he responded with wisdom. I loved that God granted him with that talent because it inspired me to become wiser. I kept speaking of my anger of peoples' immorality. My biggest question was why doesn't God change it?

Gabe spoke softly, "That is a great question. I have asked the same one but the answer is he did." I gave Gabe a curious look.

I responded, "No, I don't think that you're right. If he would have done something it wouldn't be like this."

Gabe smiled at me. "That isn't necessarily true. People don't know what they are saved from if it never happens. We don't know the days of our lives but God does. We don't know how he works either. All we do know is he does."

"Gabe, sometimes you confuse me," I said. He chuckled a little bit.

"I understand though. It's like asking a man about being saved from drowning when he never entered the water. He can't explain a situation that never occurs." Gabe nodded his head.

"Exactly!" He said with authority.

"Well, what about our problem? Why doesn't God do something about all the hatred and prison corruption? Why does he let good men die and the wicked prosper? We both know he can change it but why doesn't he?"

Gabe looked very seriously at me. He had a look on his face like he had been waiting for years for me to ask that question. He was prepared to answer it with a simple yet deep answer.

"God did do something. He sent you."

A rush of air exited my lungs. I was completely blindsided by his statement. Even more, I was humbled once again because in all my years I didn't realize how true that statement could be. When I imagined God stepping into a situation, I envisioned angels flying down from the heavens and corruption falling to its knees in agony.

I didn't see me, a weak man that has spent most of his life trapped in a prison cell. I figured that God would send great warriors into battle not someone weak as me. The Bible was packed with

David versus Goliath stories though. That gave me some reassurance. I figured God may enjoy watching the underdogs prosper. That seems to be His go to story anyway.

Gabe and I continued on with our conversation. I vented about how I felt afraid of failure and he encouraged me. I was frustrated because I tried everything that I could and I wasn't gaining any ground. In my life, it took adversity for me to realize how much I needed God. I also fought the idea that I couldn't do it on my own before I let Him in. That may be what this prison needs, it needs to be humbled so God can get back into peoples' lives.

I had several thoughts. I found myself drifting from our conversation into thinking about change. The passion I had for improving the world burned from within me. I had prayed and worked for it, but it seemed so distant. I began to think about why I wanted it so much. Why didn't I just live the rest of my life and not worry about others? A part of me felt that wasn't such a bad idea. Jesus said, *"Do not look at a sliver in another man's eye when you have a log in your own."*

The problem wasn't that I wanted change because I judged others, it was because I felt obligated that they knew they could turn their back on sin. I wanted them to know that there was an alternative lifestyle. They could choose to live a life with God as their centerpiece. I wanted people to know what it was like to live for God. That was my true goal.

If I compared myself to others I would also fall short. I remember the days when I turned my back on God but I was hurting then. Maybe that was why God chose me. He could use my experiences because I knew exactly what it was like. I could relate to others who were at a point where they believed they didn't need him. It was amazing how God worked. He could use a point in my life that I was ashamed of to bring others to Him. That was amazing all by itself.

After a while, Gabe and I began our conversation again. We decided that we wanted to have a reminder of who we serve in our cell. I didn't know why I hadn't thought of something like that before. We both wanted to have something inspirational to remind us of what we were fighting for.

I wanted a symbol of sacrifice because I felt my life was a living sacrifice. I didn't have the luxury of a normal life, but I still didn't regret where I was and what I had. I felt more honored than anything. The Lord picked me and He could have chosen anyone.

Through the perspective of a normal person, my life would look like a tragedy, like I got the short end of the stick. The amazing part was, I was one of the few people that knew what it was like to truly live. It's because God blessed me with focus.

I managed to get a little white paint from a guard. Thankfully, he was generous enough to give it to me because I had no way to pay for it. It would have cost very little but I was still poor. Gabe and I spent hours talking about what to write on the cell wall. We discussed writing a scripture but didn't have much paint, so we kept it simple. I wanted a symbol of the sacrifice Christ made for me. We both decided we would put up a cross. We looked around the cell to try to decide where to put it. I wanted it somewhere in the open so I could have a constant reminder but we didn't want to get in any trouble. Eventually, we decided to risk it and we would put it just above our cell door.

Gabe took the small jar of paint and stuck his finger into it. He carefully brushed a nearly perfect cross slightly over our cell door.

"Perfect," I said as he hopped down from the top of the sink.

I thought it was beautiful. It was a perfect contrast from the grey wall to a white cross. It was small but proportional. I felt it added a lot to our room and it made me happy.

It was the small things in prison that helped me maintain sanity. I had to look forward to all the little parts of life or I would grow depressed. That cross inspired me to stay persistent. I learned to relate parts of my life to Christ's crucifixion. I had already been at the end of a pointing finger and I knew what it felt like to be lied about. But, I was still at the point where I was carrying my cross. It was a tough journey but I couldn't give up hope because I knew I would rise again.

Chapter 20

A LOT MORE HAPPENED IN the last ten years I was in prison than the first thirty combined. There was more chaos and destruction, as well as peace and fulfillment. It felt like it took thirty years to prepare for the last few. I had to build a foundation, then a wall, and then patiently wait for the attack of my enemies.

Through my perspective, I thought I wasn't doing much but I didn't know how much was changing that I never noticed. My goal was to make a small dent in the corruption but I didn't realize that the Lord handed me a sledge hammer. I had to take a step back and get a different view before I realized how much had been accomplished. It was amazing how little by little, it was getting better.

The KPK was getting weaker and it was starting an uprising on the yard. Rival gangs were getting stronger because of a variety of things, but my goal wasn't for the KPK to be replaced. It was for the politics to get diminished as a whole. A slightly larger group was being drawn to the church but the prison as a whole started to become more on edge.

The hierarchy that the KPK held was being viewed as weak. The truth was it really hadn't weakened at all but through rumor and other means, inmates believed it had. It was mostly from the sabotage of other gangs, and the KPK believed they were too strong to be taken. It goes to show that when the untouchable lose focus, they become vulnerable.

The KPK had allowed other gangs to recruit too many and didn't stop their problems early. That was how it worked in war and it was the same in prison. With the top gang viewed as vulnerable, another would try to take the keys. It's the poison of power. Someone always wants to be on top.

The prison population started to act apprehensive. Some of the population refused to leave the safety of their personal cells. Others turned to the gang crowds for protection, so the number of gang members on the yard increased even more. For a second, it felt like everything was moving backwards. I wanted to get rid of it, not make it bigger, but sometimes things have to get worse before they get better.

I could see a lot of tension being worn on inmates' faces. People were stressing constantly. All the small things showed what was going on. Men were whispering to each other rather than talking. Others were stocking up on supplies. Even the guards could tell something was up but they were oblivious to how bad it was really getting. Even something small could have started a riot.

Then suddenly, everything changed. It was weird. It was like the calm before the storm. People were completely silent. They were not talking to each other. Few had the courage to do any of their daily activities. No one was out reading or playing cards. Everyone was watching and waiting, but no one knew when everything would go down.

I tried to live normally but it was hard. The church suffered because people didn't want to be in a vulnerable state. The worse it got, the more I saw a change in myself. I was constantly watching everybody else and their nervousness was rubbing off on me. I was concerned about everything around me.

I maintained my routine to the best of my ability but I had grown used to having a dozen people in Bible study. When it dropped to one or two people, it became difficult to get a lot of feedback. The tension went on for weeks and at the time, I hated the change.

I thought everything was worse than when I started. It's hard to explain the behavior because so many were reclusive and nothing was happening. Nobody wanted to start a riot because everyone knew a lot of lives would be lost and they didn't want that life to be their own.

Eventually, the tension dropped slightly and people became more comfortable. Inmates were still on high alert but they had been cooped up in their cells for so long they started coming out. People were back to playing cards and talking. A good part was I didn't see or hear of one fist fight because people were so worried.

I decided to seize the day and go out to the ball field for some meditation and worship. It was a nice afternoon. The sun was shining and a very few clouds covered the sky. I sat down and had my back facing the concrete wall to ensure I could sense people coming. There were more people out there than usual but by no means excessive.

There was a point in time where I felt at ease. I believed that people wouldn't mess with me while I was relaxing. That changed with the way the entire population was acting. I felt insecure about my safety so I stayed alert even while trying to relax. I saw Matthew walking toward me out of the corner of my eye. He walked up and sat down next to me. I was enjoying the beautiful day the Lord had made.

I started to talk to him but suddenly, everything erupted. I looked up into the crowd and there was an explosion of chaos. All the different gangs were charging toward each other for a giant war. I stood up instantly as all the yelling and running began. It was like the frontlines of a battle. Men were slamming into each other. Several had makeshift weapons, from sharpened toothbrushes to socks packed with dirt and rocks.

Matthew stepped behind me as the siren started blaring. Men were running in all directions. People were terrified for their lives and no one was safe. It was a different type of riot because it wasn't about the fighting. It was about letting the yard know who owned it. It was a battle to establish dominance. It was the most gruesome battle I had ever experienced.

Death and destruction surrounded me. For the first time in thirty years, I truly believed I wouldn't live through it. People were getting stabbed and beaten in every direction I looked. I turned to my side and made eye contact with a KPK member. He started rushing toward Matthew and me. I moved Matthew behind me and felt to ensure he stayed there. It wasn't only about my safety. I had to protect who I could as well. I prayed in the few seconds I had before the KPK reached us. "Lord, protect us. Send angels to watch over us today so we can continue to praise your glory."

Another KPK member followed the one headed our way. The first one came in swinging with a fury of fists. He had what looked like a sharpened bolt in his right hand. He swung toward my face as I did my best to duck and dodge. It slightly scratched me just above my eye.

I turned my face when I dodged and glimpsed at Matthew a few feet behind me. He had an intense look of fear in his eyes. I think he knew he would die. I wouldn't accept that it would all end there. It motivated me to do my best to protect him. I felt the adrenaline rush through my veins.

I turned back toward the action with an aggressive mindset. He swung his shank toward my neck and I lifted my arm to block it. I felt the metal pierce through my forearm. I was in a tough spot so I did the only thing I could. I turned and swung blindly with all my might. I could only hope to make contact. I felt the compression in my wrist as it impacted his skull. His knees wobbled as he quickly fell unconscious under my feet.

The man behind him stopped and stared at me. I pulled the shank from my forearm as I glared into his soul. He changed direction and headed toward another man across the field.

I gazed down at my forearm. It was erupting with blood. The bolt had struck into the middle of my forearm, in between the bones. The wound was horizontal and deep into my flesh, but I felt like I would be fine. The worst of it was the heavy flow of blood dripping down my forearm, off my fingertips. I couldn't feel much of my hand and could barely manage to move my fingers.

I wasn't worried about myself. My first instinct was to check and see if Matthew was okay. He rushed up next to me and stood slightly behind my side. I held my injured arm with my other hand and squeezed the wound to try to slow the bleeding. A cloud of mace went bursting through the large mob of men. It didn't do much because there were so many inmates.

It was a ruthless battle. Several men were on the ground unconscious, even dead. Others were still getting pummeled into the ground. The look of agony I saw on the faces of men was horrendous. I couldn't do anything to help them. Everything was happening fast but moving slow. I tried to analyze the situation and do whatever I could to remain safe.

I turned and looked over my shoulder. I saw Dom cornered by two rival gang members. They were moving toward him and he was in trouble. I started to step that way when suddenly, Cyrus tackled the one on the right. He started swinging his dagger into that man's face and throat. Blood splattered out of his neck with every blow. He was gone in seconds from the horrific attack. The man next to him attacked but Cyrus quickly flipped him over his back and brutally killed him too. It was as serious as a war. It was an all-out battle to the death and nearly everyone was fighting.

Dom looked traumatized. Cyrus stood up and wiped the blood off his forearm with his shirt. He looked at Dom then turned and headed back into the crowd. The look on Cyrus's face was different than most. He had a look as if he was enjoying himself, like he was excited.

The thoughts running through my head consisted of protecting those I cared about, and also those who can't protect themselves. I was doing the best I could to stop the violence and save lives. The problem was, it took violence to stop violence. It was fighting fire with fire. I was struggling because there were so many men there and I couldn't protect everyone. I would shove a man off an unconscious body just to see him attack another or me.

After the first gunshot, people still didn't stop. They didn't care if they were shot or not. They were there to make a statement to the prison population and they succeeded. The KPK wanted everyone to know that they ran the prison. To them it was about more than life and death. The sad part was they could have used their life to be committed to something more than man, but they chose otherwise.

I turned back toward the mass of the crowd. A KPK member was on top of a man punching him. He was halfway through one of his punches when the bullet knocked him over, killing him instantly.

The battle continued on only meters away from us. I pulled away from everything and concentrated on keeping Matthew and I safe. Gas canisters had been launched into the bulk of the crowd. In some places, people dispersed but continued the fight away from the gas. The prison was using all its resources to try to control the chaos. It wasn't working very well simply because the population of the prison was so much greater than the power of the guards' weapons.

A guard took a second shot and people started to bolt for the door leading back into the prison. To my surprise, it was already open. My stomach churned because that breach in security could only mean one thing. It was a takeover.

Instinctively, I headed to the door as well. I had to do my part to help. Good men would be trapped in the anarchy and I couldn't leave them stranded. My protective instinct kept me from remaining outside with the rest of the inmates. I wanted to save as many people as I could. I turned back toward Matthew and told him, "Stay put." He listened and got down on his belly like some of the other inmates. I was one of the last men to enter the building.

I rushed down the hall toward J-block. I wasn't excited for the situation going down. When I ran up to the unit, everything was chaotic. I looked into the bubble and it was empty. All the security was gone. The doors were wide open. All the inmates could roam free. It was very bad.

I felt a tickle running down my arm. I looked down and saw the blood rolling down the front of my forearm. With all the adrenaline, I had forgotten about the puncture wound. I knew before anything else I needed to stop the bleeding.

I turned away from J-block and moved down a hall to where the clinician's offices were. By blind luck, there was a nurse cart next to one of the offices. I opened the side door and there were some bandages and a wrap. I took them and went into an employee bathroom. I washed out the wound as well as I could and bandaged it up.

After I doctored myself up, I headed back to J-block. Men were yelling and screaming. Toilet paper rolls and clothes were flying across the tier. Then I saw the worst part, Sergeant Woods along with two other guards were beaten and tied at the wrist. They were seated with their backs together, supervised by an army of KPK's. I couldn't do anything to help and even if I could manage to free them, we would have nowhere to go. We were under KPK control. They controlled all the cell doors and hallways.

I went straight to my cell to make sure Gabe was okay. I walked in and he was lying on his bunk, reading a book as if nothing was going on.

I shouted, "Gabe!"

He turned toward me replying softly, "What?"

"Do you have any idea what is going on?" He looked around as if he was supposed to notice something.

"The prison has been taken over by inmates," I said.

He calmly stepped down from his bunk and walked toward the door. He looked out behind me and said, "O, wow it has."

I was flustered at the way he acted but it showed how used to chaos he had become over the years. He was completely unworried about the outside environment. After seeing him react, I realized nothing rattled Gabe. That was the best example of being calm in the storm that I had ever seen.

He became a little more serious after seeing how frantic I was.

"What should we do?" I asked.

Gabe collected his thoughts, "Probably nothing at the moment," he said.

I turned angry instantly. I started to pace around and think about how to react.

"They have hostages that need my help. I can't sit and do nothing."

I walked to the door of our cell and peered out. A lot was still going on. Men were running around yelling at the top of their lungs. The concrete jungle literally became the wild. I turned back toward Gabe.

"We have to do something!" I screamed. He was doing his best to calm me down.

"Luke, relax the worst we could do right now is make a scene. We need to stay calm so at the right moment we can try to help."

I took a deep breath and realized he was right. If we did try to help without an organized plan, then we would be outmuscled by the KPK. We needed to devise some type of plan to help get the hostages out because they were most at risk. I needed to find a way to get in touch with Sergeant Woods. I couldn't walk up and start talking to him. My best advantage was being an inmate. The KPK wouldn't know I was against them or the riot.

I stepped slightly outside my cell door and Cyrus Black was standing over by the hostages. He was holding a military shotgun that was supposed to be locked in the bubble. They used it to shoot warning shots at metal plates during fights; or in the event of a life-threating attack, they would use it on an inmate. It was different seeing it in Cyrus's hands though. A guard used it to protect but a monster like him having such a deadly weapon would only end in death.

I looked around without drawing any attention to myself. I scanned over the area to try to devise a way of getting the officers out. I looked at all the possible exits. The doors were locked so I had to get into the bubble and open one without anyone knowing. I counted the KPK members and tried to think of a high percentage way of freeing the guards. The rescue mission was going to be extremely difficult.

I hated looking over at Cyrus and the hostages. He was a very awful man. He would antagonize them by rubbing the end of the barrel on their necks as he slowly paced around them. For him, it was all about the power. He loved having the control to take any one of their lives at any moment. It disgusted me.

I couldn't bear to watch anymore because I was afraid he would pull the trigger. I couldn't imagine what they were feeling. I could see the fear in their eyes. Cyrus fed off that. I could see how much he was enjoying himself.

I turned my head away from them. If he did pull the trigger, I didn't want to witness another one of my friends being taken by that sick man. I bolted back into my cell and bumped into Gabe. He was watching everything going on.

"This is not good," I said very softly. He acknowledged me with a graceful nod. "Not good, not good at all," he responded.

The more I thought, the more I realized that I couldn't take on the KPK single-handedly. My only rational option would be to try to signal help to get police inside the prison. I had an awful feeling that it would all end in a bloodbath. I needed some serious help to have any part of it turn out well.

I walked back out into the dayroom to do more recon. As I was standing there, I could hear the scratching sound of the guards' radios and then some muddling of voices. The police would have no idea of how many hostages they had or what was going on in the unit. They were blind.

Cyrus must have heard the radios too because he walked over and took the radio from Sergeant Woods. I moved closer so I could listen, but not so close that I would draw any attention. With all the commotion going on, no one seemed to care what I was doing. They were enjoying the freedom of roaming around J-block with no offi-cers instructing them on what to do.

I heard Cyrus speak into the radio. I couldn't make out exactly what he was saying but he was smiling as he talked. It was still loud in the unit so I moved even closer and sat down against a wall and listened. He looked at me but I looked away and nothing was said.

I listened without looking at him and tried to gather as much info as possible.

"I am the one running the show," he said.

I could hear the officer on the other end of the line talking back. He was saying everything that Cyrus wanted to hear.

"Yes, you're the boss. You're in control but what can we give you for the officers?" He stood there with a confused look as if he hadn't thought of making any demands.

I thought the takeover was a very organized attack but at that moment, I realized he really didn't think everything through. I think that his initial plan was to make a statement but it turned into a lot more.

"I want my freedom," he replied. My heart sank. I was sure my face turned slightly pale too. I couldn't imagine them letting a psychopath like him out. I was sure that they felt the same way though.

"Okay, we will talk it over," the officer replied.

Cyrus turned enraged instantly. I think he knew they would never let him free. The fact they would even consider letting him out made him think they weren't taking him seriously.

His face flourished red and the vein on his forehead started to swell. I could see how angry he was. I had watched men like this for a lifetime and I knew how they thought. His fuse was instant and the pettiest of circumstances set him off. My stomach churned as he dropped the radio and walked toward a hostage. He kicked him over, pressed the gun against the officer's head, and pulled the trigger.

Chapter 21

THE SOUND OF THE GUN going off sent a shockwave through my body. Everyone on the tier looked over at the body on its side. I was really scared, not for myself, but for the lives of others. He would kill anyone and everyone if given the chance. That is just the way he was wired. He was a psychopath and killing made him feel powerful.

Two KPK members walked over without being told a word. They grabbed the body and carried it off. They dragged him out like he was a dead deer. I felt so bad for that man's family. They would have no idea at the time that he was already gone. They would hope and pray for his safety but it was already too late.

I felt so helpless. If I were to make a move, then I would end up dead as well. I really needed some help, so I prayed. I made one of the most crucial prayers of my entire life, at the same time it was also one of the simplest.

I simply said in my mind, "God, we need you. God, I need you." The helplessness was draining my morale. Lack of hope is one of the devil's greatest weapons. He stole my optimism for the moment but I was reminded by that little voice in my head. *"Have faith."*

The fear on the faces of the hostages had spiked. They realized how much more trouble they were actually in. Even some of the inmates were shocked at Cyrus's instant reaction to kill. I think the worst part was how the KPK members reacted afterwards. They walked the corpse off as if they were taking garbage to the dumpster. I don't think the police understood the true nature of these men.

I decided it was now or never. Even if I lost my life, at least I would lose it in the hope of saving someone else. It would be a noble way to die. I didn't have time to devise a plan, I just had to act.

Cyrus was laughing at the fear of Sergeant Woods and the other guard. Cyrus wanted to torture them. He didn't feel remorse for his actions. He enjoyed the suffering of others. He walked up to Sergeant Woods and looked down at him. Then he turned to the man next to the sergeant. He brought his fist back and struck him so hard that his feet left the ground as he impacted his head. The man flew back and fell on his shoulders. He rolled over gasping for air. The punch was so hard I felt I couldn't breathe either.

I wanted to protect him. I reacted without thinking. I couldn't stand back and watch. I walked up to my greatest enemy.

"Stop!" I yelled.

Cyrus turned his head toward me. He added a crooked smile to his face as he responded. "And, why should I do that?" I looked down toward Sergeant Woods. The terror in his face ate at my soul.

"They are hostages. If you kill them then you won't have anything to negotiate with. The police don't care about us. They will want the guards." He looked at me while he was thinking. He turned back and looked at the guard who was still panting from the blow he just took.

Cyrus stepped closer to the guard. He looked at me again and then back down. He suddenly lifted his foot and started to stomp violently on the semi-conscious guard, blow after violent blow onto his head. The man screamed at first but after a few hits he went silent. That didn't stop Cyrus for a second. He stomped his head into the concrete well past death.

"One guard is good enough," he said as he wiped his bloody boot on the ground.

Cyrus slowly walked up in front of me. He stood there and looked me up and down. Then he put his disgusting, vile hand on my shoulder.

"I will make the decisions, preacher man."

I was sick to my stomach. It didn't matter how many encounters I had with death it didn't get any easier. At every moment I grew more and more hopeless. The more I tried to help the worse Cyrus made it. I stepped back away from him to try to keep myself safe.

Cyrus started to talk to me, "I still don't understand why he did it?" I looked at him with a confused look.

"Jesse was a coward. There was no room for the weak anyway," he said.

I was even more confused than before. I stuttered slightly, "What? What do you mean?"

Cyrus looked at me with his empty, evil eyes. "You don't know? Jesse was ordered to kill you. I gave him the choice either the KPK or this God you preach about. He chose wrongly, so I showed him who really has the power."

The thoughts crossing my mind were unexplainable. I had no idea what Jesse had actually sacrificed. He gave his life for me and I never knew it. I remembered he said he had to step out to protect someone but I didn't know it was me. It was noble. He didn't do it for praise or glory. He did it because he wanted God over everything else.

I turned my head back at Cyrus. I had a different look in my eyes than before. It was war—good versus evil. I had vowed my life in prison to destroying the evil that destroyed others. This was my chance. I was going to stop the KPK or die trying.

The negotiator spoke back over the radio. "Mr. Black, what is going on in there? Are the hostages alright?"

Cyrus grabbed the radio as he looked at Sergeant Woods. He turned his head and looked at the guard lying lifeless on the ground.

"Yeah, all three are fine," he lied.

I had a glimpse of hope cross my mind. Cyrus made my work easier by letting the police know how many hostages he had. I noticed him slip the information but Cyrus didn't skip a beat. He was arrogant and believed he was untouchable. I had to be able to use that against him. If I played into his ego then maybe I could still get Sergeant Woods out alive.

"Let me speak to the hostages." Cyrus walked up next to Sergeant Woods who had tears in his eyes from the fear. Cyrus rested the barrel of the gun on Sergeant Woods's neck.

"Lie," he whispered.

He held up the radio to his mouth. Sergeant Woods erupted in a panic and started crying. Cyrus started to smile as Sergeant Woods whimpered. After a few seconds, he regained his composure and started to speak.

"This is Sergeant Gary Woods," he stuttered.

"I'm a hostage along with Corporal Todd and Corporal Keko. I'm the only one—alive."

Cyrus ripped the radio away from Sergeant Woods's face. The look Cyrus had on his face was complete shock. He couldn't believe that the fear he held over Sergeant Woods hadn't given him total control. I think that was the biggest reason Sergeant Woods panicked. It was because he thought he would surely die from saying what he was about to say.

I almost felt I had to smirk. My friend showed his bravery and stuck it to the man at the same time. Cyrus backhanded Sergeant Woods and stormed off in a rage. The sergeant looked up at me after he hit the ground. He too had a crooked smile—a crooked, bloody smile.

I don't think he realized that his actions probably saved his life. Cyrus was mesmerized by the fact someone didn't disintegrate under the fear of him. The curiosity of why he didn't crumble was probably what kept Cyrus from killing him.

I walked off toward my cell with that slight smile still on my face. I stepped into the cell to talk to Gabe. He wasn't doing much at the moment. It was a waiting game. I couldn't do anything to help the situation until the time was right.

It was ironic that in a situation like I was in the best thing to do was to remain calm and do normal things. I took that moment to brush up on some reading. I sat up on my bunk and read some of my Bible. It comforted me in some of the most devastating situations. I was still distracted by everything going on. I kept getting off my bunk and checking on Sergeant Woods. He was sitting up against the cinder block wall with a few KPK members standing guard.

I lost track of where Cyrus ran off to. Honestly, I didn't really care. I felt like I had to let go of what evil he had put in my life. I had to put him behind me and move on. Every time I thought of what he had done to my life, it would cloud my thinking. I had to remain focused on the situation and remain optimistic. God gifted me with a positive outlook and I planned on using that gift. I felt that death itself couldn't take that away.

Several hours had passed. The majority of the riot had subsided. People were still doing what they wanted to do but most of them did what they would on a normal day. The difference was, they didn't have a guard breathing down their neck. I knew eventually something would happen and life would go back to normal, so I felt I had to ride it out.

I heard some clunking as if a can was tossed on the concrete. I heard it again a couple more times. I moved toward my door and opened it slightly. Smoke was erupting out of the cans. Men were coughing and running into the cells, slamming them shut. I looked through the smoke and saw Cyrus pulling Sergeant Woods up by his armpit.

He was yelling at his people, giving orders. I saw policemen coming in from the other side of the tier. They were dressed in black body armor with helmets and riot shields. The men behind them had assault rifles. Cyrus had his shotgun in hand and was pulling Sergeant Woods into K-block. This was the moment I had been waiting for. I reacted instantly and bolted after them. I had to save Sergeant Woods.

A few other inmates were already ahead of me rushing through the door. The door that separated the pods was shutting. I sprinted a little faster. I was pushing my body to its limits. I turned my head to the side and noticed I was running right next to a KPK. He was striding step for step with me. The door was nearly closed. There was no way both of us would make it through. I reached out my arm and shoved him on the shoulder. He smashed head first into the concrete wall. I turned my body and lunged through the doorway. I barely managed to squeeze through the gap as the door closed behind me.

I stood up off the ground. The door was shut and I could hear men pounding their fists on the other side of the steel door. I actually felt bad shoving that guy into the wall but I had to save my friend. The way I saw it was that was one less to Cyrus's army. I looked around and Cyrus was nowhere in sight. A couple KPK members looked back at me but didn't give me much attention. They may have wondered what the loud thud was from when I came through the doorway but they didn't give me any more attention than a glance.

I was more out of my territory than I had ever felt before. I had never stepped foot in KPK territory. A few other guys had come through that didn't have any gang affiliations either so that helped take some pressure off me. I was still with the most ruthless portion of the prison population and that was never easy.

I looked around the tier and I knew this was going to be the final battlefield. All the KPK members were suiting up for war. I was scared. The chances were, once the KPK attacked the guards, they would shoot us all. It wouldn't matter if we were part of it or not. It was them or us, and we were just a bunch of inmates. To the public, they would justify it. They would say we already had our chance or they had no choice but to put us all down. But I was still there because I couldn't live with myself unless I did everything possible to save Sergeant Woods. I had to find him as quickly as possible and get out before the anarchy started.

I walked through the tier taking every step cautiously. The mood of the men around me was changing. They started shouting. It was like war cries. They were pumping themselves up. They packed the entrances of the tier to build a barricade. It was a war tactic to limit the amount of police entering the tier.

They were prepared for battle with their broomsticks and shanks. I thought it was suicidal but to them it was about honor and brotherhood. I still wished they would put that type of commitment into something more productive than violence.

I made my way across the tier. I saw men going in and out of a cell in the corner of the unit. I moved toward it but kept enough space to keep from looking nosy. I found a good angle and peered in. Cyrus was in there talking to a couple men. Sergeant Woods was there sitting right behind him tied at the wrist and leaning against the concrete.

The war was coming soon. The KPK had no intention of going down without a fight. They started the uprising and were going to finish it. Negotiations obviously didn't go well for Cyrus. That worried me even more because it made Sergeant Woods expendable. Cyrus had nothing to lose anymore. He would already be sentenced to death for murdering the guards that is if he lived through the riot at all.

I heard an explosion of yelling and looked over at the door I first entered. It was opening. Several smoke canisters were shot onto the tier. As the door opened, policemen with riot shields started to move through. The KPK smashed into them. The war had begun.

Chapter 22

CYRUS AND THE OTHER MEN bolted out of the cell. I seized the opportunity. I rushed in and started to untie Sergeant Woods's wrists. I stood him up so we could get out of the tier away from the war. He started to say thanks when the look of relief on his face suddenly switched to panic. I slowly turned my head to look behind me. It was Cyrus standing at the cell door with a murderous look on his face.

He was holding his shotgun in his right hand. He smiled slightly as he raised his hand. I reacted instantly and lunged at him. I pushed him at the shoulder and the barrel of the gun swung under my armpit as it went off. He fell slightly from the impact but managed to remain upright. I ripped at the shotgun and pulled it from his grip. I pulled so hard it flew from my hand and slid across the ground. It slid back into the cell I was just in. We both moved toward the shotgun as our fist fight began. He shoved at me and I fell on my side.

He lost his balance from the push and was crawling toward the gun. I stood back up and jumped on top of him as he reached his hand out. His fingers were barely out of reach from the stock of the gun. We rolled over and he struck me on the top of my head. We turned over again and I struck back.

I swung several times as he protected his face with his forearms. Out of the corner of my eye, I saw a body slouched over in the cell. I gazed up into the cell and saw Sergeant Woods up against the concrete. He wasn't moving, even in the slightest, and blood started to puddle away from his body.

I lost concentration for that slight moment and Cyrus took advantage of the situation. He bucked me off his body and I fell to the side. I caught myself with my hand and stood up. Cyrus stood up too and brought his fist up to his chin. We started circling with the gun a few feet out of both of our reaches.

He gestured at me to attack. I stepped toward him and swung. He ducked and hit me extremely hard in the ribs. I brought my arm over his head and grabbed hold of him. We shuffled around and fell back to the ground. He was on top of me swinging left and right. My good arm was pinned under his leg. I used all my strength to protect my head with my wounded forearm. The pain was excruciating from every blow to my arm and head.

I turned side to side trying to push him off but it wasn't working. I couldn't do anything to get him off me. Consciousness was starting to slip away. Then suddenly, I slipped into a dreamlike state. Everything turned blurry but I could still make out Cyrus's body. I could see his fists move away and toward me.

The state of bliss I had experienced those few times in my life was back. I had no pain or worries. Then I couldn't see anything but white. It was blinding flash but it didn't go away. Nothing mattered to me anymore. Life seemed to be perfect. I wasn't afraid of my future or my past. It was about the now and nothing else.

I knew I was still under Cyrus, experiencing every strike he had thrown. It was odd because it didn't matter to me. I only cared about the grace my soul was saturated in. I only felt peace and hope. It felt like I was there for a lifetime. The bliss and comfort was so great I didn't want to lose it. I wanted to stay forever but something told me I wasn't done yet. The white was fading out and I couldn't remember much of what happened while I was in that dreamlike trance.

Reality set back in. I could see the blurry version of Cyrus slugging away at my body. He moved slowly as he pulled each fist back into view and continued striking me. Everything seemed slower. I turned my head and saw the KPK members keeping the guards back in the doorway. Only a sliver of time had actually past.

I had lost faith, not in God, but in the enemy. I knew the enemy would not win. The devil was already defeated. I can't explain how I knew that or what told me that, but just that it was the truth. I talked to God and he answered back without ever saying a word. I trusted Him and He always came through.

I thrust my hips up as hard as I could. Cyrus toppled over the top of me. I moved with perfect precision and quickness. Everything around me was still a gaze but I took advantage of it moving slowly. I could think and reacted faster than everything around me. I was moving with swiftness and power. I never knew I had that type of strength.

I jumped on top of Cyrus and crawled up his legs. I got on top and struck him several times. He tried to move but he felt so weak to me. I didn't want to hurt him but I had to stop him. He turned over and I struck him a few more times. His eyes were swelling and he didn't move as much. He finally lowered his hands and I stopped swinging. I stood up over the top of him. He was still breathing but the rest of his body was still. I walked over next to the cell door and picked up the shotgun lying on the ground.

I walked back over to him. I was standing at the feet of his body. The gun was in my hand pointed at the ground. He opened his eyes and looked up at me. The opportunity was there. I was finally in a position where I could take vengeance on my enemy. He deserved the punishment. He killed and destroyed the lives of good men. They were my friends and for once I could be the hero. I could provide them justice.

He looked at the gun in my hand and then back up into my eyes.

"Do it!" He said.

I lifted the shotgun up at him. I felt my finger glide over the trigger. As I squeezed, I felt the tension of the trigger push back against me. My judgment was cloudy. I feared if I was doing the right thing.

He had just tried to kill me. He had taken so much and deserved to die. I wanted to take revenge on my enemy.

Then suddenly, the voice in my head reminded me, vengeance wasn't mine to take. I took a deep breath and dropped my arm to the side. I let the gun slip off the tip of my fingers onto the floor. I was so exhausted. My knees wobbled and my head throbbed from the terrible beating I had taken. I couldn't pull the trigger. It was about more then what I wanted. It was about the message. If I could forgive someone like Cyrus for all the pain he had caused, then I could forgive anyone. And if I can forgive anyone, I can show others how to forgive everyone.

Most people still wouldn't understand. They looked at what occurred through worldly eyes. They could justify the situation. They could bring up the point that he was the worst type of person or that he deserved to die, but for me I didn't feel that it was my duty to do it. I knew God wanted me to show mercy and prove that forgiveness was for everyone. That was the message from the beginning. Everyone can be part of the forgiveness of Christ because everyone needs it.

By the time I dropped the gun, the police had broken through. I was still panting from exhaustion when they ran up.

"Get on the ground!" They yelled repetitively.

Before I had a chance to move, they tackled me. They handcuffed me and a cop stood on top of me with a knee in my back. I turned my head and peered into the cell to see Sergeant Woods. He was surrounded by a few paramedics. His shirt was soaked in blood but it looked like it had started at his shoulder. His eyes were open and he looked at me. He couldn't say anything but the look in his eyes said, "Thank you." I couldn't explain it but I knew he would be okay.

I had a different perspective this time around. For the first time in my life, the cold concrete floor felt good. I embraced it and pressed my cheek against the ground, thankful for the day to be over, thankful for every blessing God had given me.

Chapter 23

LIFE AFTER THE RIOT TOOK a little while to go back to normal. The security in the prison increased and the day to day violence subsided. The punishment for fist fighting and gang activity increased and it deterred a lot from happening. They decided to build a new prison strictly for segregation and it helped to ship out the worst of people.

Prison life got better and the warden even added incentives if inmates behaved. Sometimes in life it takes chaos for change and sometimes that chaos is worth the reward. It was awesome to be able to sit down and eat dinner without an argument leading to a fist fight. It was the small things that people end up taking for granted.

After life started to get back to normal, I restarted my routine. I prepared a sermon to preach and continued my Bible study. The church changed after the riot. More people turned to God rather than each other. Most men needed help, not punishment. I wish I could've sent that message to judges that were quick to condemn.

I walked back into my cell after a typical study session. I started small talk with Gabe about how his day was and what he did. Our conversation shifted back to the past. We talked a little about the riot. I found it hysterical that Gabe spent the majority of the riot being carefree on his bunk. It suited him so well to have zero worries in the mists of trouble.

We spent the rest of the evening talking about life and memories like we usually would. The next day I saw a familiar face that lifted my spirit sky high. It was Sergeant Woods. I hadn't seen him since the riot but I heard that he spent nearly a month in the hospital. I was relieved to see him though. He walked up to me.

"How are you doing?" I asked.

"I'm good," He smiled

"That's great news. I'm glad that you're back to normal." I couldn't get the smile off my face. It stretched cheek to cheek but I was just so happy to see him.

"I came here to thank you, Luke. If you wouldn't have acted so heroically, I wouldn't be here today. My life as a prison guard is officially over so I had to come here as a visitor. I just wanted to thank you for everything you did."

I chuckled and said, "Well, what are friends for." We both bust up laughing.

We talked for a while. I wanted to hear about how he was doing and what his plans were. He showed me the scar on his shoulder from the shotgun. It was good to have a friend that wasn't trapped in these walls with me. After a while, his tone changed. He became a little more serious.

"I need to tell you about Cyrus Black," he said.

"What about him?" I asked.

"Well, he was arraigned for murder and initiating a riot. After court, the guards were doing their rounds and they found him dead in his cell. He had hung himself and I figured you should know."

"I don't really know what to say. It's a shock to hear that," I replied.

"You don't need to say anything. Just take in the information and go on."

Sergeant Woods left and I felt lost. I didn't know how I really felt about the death of Cyrus. In a lot of ways, I felt Cyrus got off easy. He stole so many lives, even his own. He would have spent decades locked up suffering by himself but in a way I was relieved. When I put that gun down, it symbolized something for me. I forgave him for everything he did. I didn't want him to suffer even though he inflicted so much pain. It was a mindset from God and I was thankful he gave it to me.

I went back to church to preach for the first time since the takeover. I saw several familiar faces, including Dom and Matthew. They both made it through the riot without any harm. I moved up to the altar and stared down at the sermon I had prepared. I wanted to speak but not much would come out. I felt all the emotions I had for years bottled up inside me.

One emotion separated from the rest and took my mood with it. It was relief. I was so relieved that after everything that occurred my fight was finally over. Prison politics were still around but to a different magnitude. With the new prison being built and the Gang Task Force being developed, it changed everything. They didn't tolerate anything. The random beatings stopped and people weren't posted at the corner of their territory anymore. They sent fighters and men with gang affiliations to segregation. After that, they didn't want to represent anymore. They just wanted to do their own time.

I looked up at the men still shuffling into the chapel. More and more kept piling through the doorway. Before I knew it, the place was packed and still more men were walking in. In my entire time preaching, I never had a crowd so big. I decided to go impromptu and speak from the heart.

"Life isn't always fair. It isn't always what we want it to be or what we think it should be. Every man in here understands what it feels like to get the short end of the stick. But focusing on that part of our lives only holds us back. If you're constantly looking behind then you can't see what is in front of you. It is like walking backwards, you can still move but you won't have any direction.

My message is turn around. See what God has laid out for you. If you are searching for fulfillment, then look to Christ. Sprint into His arms and He will embrace you. If you're looking for healing you can find it with God. If you need forgiveness, love, or security, God has it all. He has given every one of us so many blessings but some people can't see them because they refuse to look. Just turn around.

I know what it feels like to be lost. My life has been torn to bits time and time again, but God has always helped me pick up the pieces. I tried anger to mask my own pain. I tried to fulfill myself, by myself, but none of it worked.

Only God can fill the void in your soul. Those who feel it know what I'm talking about. It's that pit in your chest that burns from within and that thought of asking, "Is this all life has to offer?" I promise there is so much more to life but you have to get started. It starts with Christ as your cornerstone, so don't be afraid anymore. The time to accept Jesus is now. Stand up and take the first step toward Christ. It is the most important step you will ever take."

Some men started crying. I rarely felt I spoke to such a magnitude that men would change everything because of my words. I think it was because for the first time, it was okay to let some of that emotion out. It influenced several inmates to let go and let God. Also, I felt when I stepped in front of the pulpit, God spoke, and He has very powerful words.

I let God speak through me and tell these hurting men what they needed to hear. I asked, "Does anyone here wish to be saved?" I heard a loud, "I do!" and I watched Dom walk down the middle of the chapel to the pulpit. Men started to follow his lead. Rival gang members walked side by side to Christ.

More and more kept coming. I wanted to cry because it was literally a dream come true. No longer would I have to worry about their salvation. They wanted their freedom and Jesus was the only one that could set them free. The most beautiful part was that He did.

Chapter 24

IT WAS A NORMAL DAY about seven and a half years after the riot. I was called by the tier officer to go to the attorney room. I didn't know what for because I didn't have an attorney. I still listened and went there because of my curiosity. I walked into the room and there was a man sitting down reading a paper. As I walked in, he stood up and reached out his hand to me. We shook hands and he introduced himself.

"Hello, I am Mr. Barnes," he said.

We both sat down and I'm sure I had a look of curiosity on my face. He responded politely to my mood.

"I'm sure you are curious to why we are having this meeting to begin with," he said. I nodded back at him.

"Yeah?" I said with a curious look.

"I will get straight to the point. I did some investigation into this case because it was brought to me by a friend. There is some new evidence and testimony that could result in your conviction being overturned and the possibility of your release."

I gasped for air. I had only dreamed of hearing those words. I literally pinched my arm to make sure I wasn't dreaming and I was actually in reality. I had given up on freedom a very long time ago. I didn't know what it would be like to be free. I had been in prison nearly forty years. I was considered an old man even though I still felt young.

I wanted to cry but I kept my composure.

"What is the new evidence?" I asked. He looked into my eyes.

"We have a confession and a murder weapon. We are waiting on the DNA results from the weapon and we have a taped confession. With this much hard evidence I could see a high possibility of your release," he said.

At that point, I couldn't hold the tears from coming. I believed that I would be set free. I didn't know when, but I believed it was coming. I had so many questions I wanted to ask. The biggest one in my mind was who really did it?

"Who confessed?" I asked.

"It was a name you are probably familiar with because he testified at your trial." He looked down at a piece of paper and read through it quickly.

"It was a Mr. Evans. He was a detective in your case," he said.

I thought someone in the D.A. office had done it, I just didn't know who. He knew I was innocent the entire time and still left me locked up. He was such coward.

"I want to confront him when this is all over," I said a little aggressively.

"Well, that would be quite difficult."

"Why's that?" I asked.

"Well, he passed away. Part of his will was this tape being sent to the D.A. office with the confession and murder weapon. A copy was also sent to my friend, a retired attorney, to prevent any cover up and that all led to where we are now."

My mind was racing. So much new information had been gathered and I had a sense of relief. I was excited to have hope again but for the moment I only wanted to gather the information.

"Can I watch the tape?" I asked.

"Yes, I brought a copy in case you wanted to watch it," he said. He reached into his bag and pulled out a thin, gray box. He opened it and it had a screen on it. It was the first time I had seen anything like it.

"What is that?" I asked. He smiled at me.

"This is a laptop computer," he said a little jokingly.

I was so amazed. He hit a button and the screen lit up. I had heard about technology from people coming into the prison but this was the first time I had actually seen it. I never really thought about the development of the outside world. It was never relevant because I thought I wouldn't see it again. I was starting to become scared. *What if I couldn't manage to be part of the outside world again?*

I didn't know how anything worked. I knew nothing about computers or technology. I started to shake from the fear. I never thought I would be scared to be set free. I didn't know anyone out there. Then scripture took control of my thoughts. I still had God and He would provide. That calmed me down tremendously.

Mr. Barnes started the video. "Hello, I am Carl Evans." He looked so much older than I remembered. He was sitting on a couch looking into the camera. There was a date running across the bottom part of the screen. The video I was watching was eleven years old. That got my blood boiling even more because if he would have come forth with the video back then, I would have been freed over a decade ago.

"If you are watching this, then I must have passed. I truly apologize for the delay in this information but I couldn't justify losing my freedom and basically my life. I know it is selfish and I am sorry. I wish I was a stronger person but I didn't think I could handle prison. However, I want whoever is watching to know that I am going to tell the complete truth. I finally have to do the right thing and come clean."

I crunched my teeth together. I felt even angrier. He could have set me free and his reason for not doing so was because it was him or me. Man truly has a selfish nature and I hated being a victim of it.

He continued on. "I want this testimony to be official by the court of the law." He then pulled out a Bible and showed it to the camera. He placed his hand on the Bible and raised his right hand. "I do solemnly swear to tell the truth, the whole truth, and nothing but the truth so help me God. I also for the record would like to inform you that I am under no outside influence. I am doing this by my own free will. I am in the right state of mind and I am doing this because it is the right thing to do."

He looked straight into the camera. I felt like he was trying to look directly at me. "I'm here to inform the courts that Mr. Luke Cassidy is an innocent man. He was convicted of first degree murder and sentenced to life in prison. I want to inform the court that I am the true perpetrator. The case was set up by me in order to clear myself of the conviction. I want to give the court my complete confession and some hard evidence to back it up as well."

He pulled out a knife in a sealed plastic bag. It was thin and about six inches long. "This is the true murder weapon. It has had no manipulation. It has the blood of the victim, Jean Cooper. It has my finger prints as well. I sealed it after the murder in the case that the guilt would build so much that I would have to turn myself in. It will be sent with a copy of this confession to the D.A. Office in the event of my death."

I didn't know what to think at that point. I was on the fence between joy of my probable release and anger because this man was such a coward that he could let an innocent man pay the price for his crime.

"I want to share my testimony to the murder itself. I will share my motive, the truth about the crime, and everything I did to set up the case to keep myself from being a suspect. I do want to inform the viewers of the video that it will be slightly graphic because I want to be specific as possible. I want there to be no confusion to my guilt. I am one hundred percent guilty and the man incarcerated today, Luke Cassidy, is not even the slightest of a percent to blame."

I felt relieved to hear him say that. Finally, someone else knew for certain that I had told the truth from the beginning. "I will start with the motive of my crime. This was a planned attack that had no relation to the victim but to her father. I was paid to stop his campaign for governor. I was in a bad place with some bad people and I had to get the money to save my own life. I got an offer and was told to distract him with this horrific crime, so I did it."

It was all about politics and money? I asked myself. He ruined my life because of something like that. It was to come up on the dollar bill. I was betrayed by society for monetary gain. The irony was it reminded me of someone.

"I want to tell the viewers about what I did in regards to the victim. I kidnapped her using my detective car. I told her who I was and that it was very important she come with me. She listened to me after I showed her my badge and got into the car. She asked what was going on and I lied to her saying we needed to ask her some questions.

I drove to the outskirts of town. No one was around and I pulled her from the car. She screamed but there was no one there to hear her. I pulled the knife I had from its sheath and I stabbed her multiple times in the neck. It did not last long and I didn't draw out the pain. I stopped stabbing when I knew she was gone."

He was crying by that point in his confession. I could see the years of remorse and guilt in his face. For a second, I actually felt sorry for him. He was emotionally bound by what he did this entire time but it didn't justify his actions. That was an awful thing to do to someone else. Adding what he did to me just made it worse. That is how the devil worked. He will take a spark and turn it into a forest fire. It can start with one small lie and then to cover that lie he would have to lie again. Before he knows it, the entire forest had burned down and several lives are destroyed. I could see what had happened.

"The day after the murder, I had to find someone to pin it on. I used my power as a detective to look into resent injuries at the hospital and only one came up for the day. It was a knife wound so I had to take advantage of the opportunity. It was Luke Cassidy or me, so I chose myself. He was a young kid with no criminal record but I knew how to manipulate the system.

I took the body in my car and drove up to where the medical report said his accident occurred. I knew I found the exact spot when

I saw the knife in the turnoff by the side of the road and dried up blood on the oak tree right behind it. I took her body out of the car and hid it back behind the tree in some brush.

I made sure nothing on her body could tie me to the murder. I closely examined her entire body and removed everything I could. After that, I drove back into town and sealed the knife I used for the murder in a plastic bag. Then I hid it in the insulation of my roof. I cleaned my car very thoroughly before I went back to the station. They were just getting ready to send a search party out for the girl.

I told D.A. Green that I pulled the medical records from the E.R. which is standard protocol in case she was at the hospital. I told him about Luke Cassidy having a knife wound and if it was a homicide we should check every avenue. The search party found the body conveniently at the same place of Luke's accident. That led to the arrest and conviction.

I also lied at his trial. I said what was needed to make sure he was convicted. I pushed the case to trial so it would close quickly and it all worked. No one ever suspected me but I always knew what I had done. It was the worst thing I ever did in my entire life. I almost came clean several times but I couldn't justify losing everything. I wish I could take it back but I can't. If Luke Cassidy is still alive by the time this video is seen, I want him to know I am truly sorry."

He was looking right at me when he said that. I instantly broke down. I was sobbing uncontrollably. The pain of all my loss was from what he did to me. My parents died because of what he did to me. My freedom, my life, everything was gone from what he did to me.

I argued with myself. From second to second, my feelings about him changed. I wanted to forgive him and hate him at the same time. It took such evil to live a life like he did. I felt if he would have been truly sorry, he would have told the truth sooner. It made sense to me. How could he be sorry and not let the truth out? He chose the path of a coward. He waited to die before he would finally confess. He suffered no consequences on earth for what he did.

I was so angry at him. I was angry at myself too. I knew in my heart what I had to do but I didn't want to. I wanted to hate but I knew that would only give the devil a foothold. Instead, I just kept crying. I tried not to think about anything. I simply let all my bottled up emotion release. My years of frustration and confusion were being left at the table.

After the video ended, I just sat there. Mr. Barnes told me he would give me a moment to be alone and walked out of the attorney room. I had an epic battle going throughout my mind. I knew what I was going to do because it was time for me to be completely free and hate is a prison of its own. I prayed to God thanking Him for everything He did for me. The ability to finally put it all behind and to truly forgive those who trespass against us is a gift.

I forgave him, not because I truly felt he deserved it, but because my Father had forgiven me for so much more. I didn't have to but I wanted to. Society would have completely understood if I had picked to hate him, but the ironic part was they couldn't grasp how I could forgive him. It is something people will only understand if they decide to pick up their own cross and follow the road less traveled.

Chapter 25

WHEN I WALKED BACK INTO my cell, I had a bittersweet feeling. Part of me knew it was time for the next chapter of my life. The other was sad because my best friend in the entire world wasn't coming with me.

I told Gabe everything about my meeting with the attorney. I told him that I had a hearing coming up in a few days for the new evidence and it was likely that I will be set free. With all the news I was telling him, his smile kept getting bigger and bigger. He was so happy for me. I wanted to believe if the tables were turned that I would feel the same way for him. I would but at the same time, I wouldn't want to lose him from my life.

He was always by my side. I wish I could have seen the world through his eyes. I never saw him angry in my entire life. In the worst of times, he happily smiled and kept positive. He lifted my spirits when I was down and he suffered with me through my pain. Most importantly, he loved me. It was unconditional brotherly love. He didn't judge me from a wicked part of my past but he stood by me to see a better future. I was going to miss him more than anything in the world.

We sat in the cell talking for hours. We laughed so hard about the stupidest of subjects. He made fun out of how much trouble I would have with all the new technology on the streets. I had seen stuff on the television but I didn't understand it much.

It still led to some good laughs. We just talked and I cherished the moment. It was a lot like the way it was when I first met him.

Most of the time I spent with Gabe was simply talking to each other. I had such a strong brotherly love for Gabe. After nearly forty years, I still felt I hadn't spent enough time with him. He was a true gentleman and I was grateful to have had the experience of knowing him.

The next day, I was transferred to the county jail and sat in solitary waiting for my appeal hearing. I woke up in the morning to a guard telling me it was time for court. The jail was under the courthouse so I had to walk up the stairs to get there. I will always remember the sound the shackles made from striking the concrete on the way up. I gripped the rail beside me and took my time with every step. Once I reached the top, I took a deep breath as they opened the door to the courtroom.

There was hardly anyone there. Behind the prosecutor was empty besides a single reporter at the very back. It was so different than everything I remembered about my trial. I was expecting evil eyes to be glaring down at me because that was what I was familiar with. I had no idea who the judge or prosecutor was. The only person that had been at the original trial was me.

Mr. Barnes nodded his head at me as I walked in. I walked up next to him and sat down. I expected it to be the same as before but it wasn't. I grew used to disappointment so I was ready for them to tell me the video wasn't admissible or something had ruined the appeal. Honestly, I was expecting it to happen.

Everyone looked different. The clothes they wore and their hair. The judge was a tall, white man with grey hair. To me, judges tended to all look the same. The prosecutor was a woman this time. She had short black hair and seemed nice. She didn't glare at me as I entered the room. I was scared because everything was so much different than what I had remembered.

Then the judge started to speak. Finally, something familiar. He worded his sentences like a judge would. "Hello, we are here today to hear oral argument on the appeal of case, State vs. Luke J. Cassidy. I will render my decision on the case at the end of the hearing. I will start by asking the prosecution and defense if there are any issues on whether we can proceed with the case today." Mr. Barnes shook his head and so did the prosecutor. The judge spoke, "Okay, we will begin. Mrs. Gartner, you have the floor." She nodded her head as she stacked some papers.

"Thank you, Your Honor. I will begin with my opening. This case is very old. In fact, I was barely born at the time it occurred. The fact still is Mr. Cassidy was convicted of first degree murder. He was also sentenced to life without the possibility of parole.

This is a very serious conviction and the state feels that video evidence is not sufficient enough to overturn the conviction. The state feels with the amount of time Mr. Cassidy has spent, he would not be suitable to reenter society. He has lived most of his life behind bars and the state feels he wouldn't cope outside of prison walls."

I kept thinking to myself, *Here we go again.* For a moment, I didn't mind because I had a sense of familiarity. Prosecutors have a way of taking a situation and looking for any way to win. It could be blatantly obvious that a defendant isn't guilty but they still look for some way to get the conviction. That was my experience with prosecutors anyway.

I decided to take that experience and change it up though. Instead of focusing on the negative of what the prosecutor had to say, I decided to put that type of insight into the positive of my situation. I looked for what I could be thankful for. I smiled as I thought to myself, *At least I have a chance. I could be sitting in my cell with no change but at least I get to experience something new.* I feel it is important to always remain optimistic, to always hold on to hope.

The prosecutor talked for a while but I managed to tune her out. She argued the tape shouldn't be admissible because she couldn't cross examine the witness. She threw in other cases with similarities. I just sat in my chair taking the impact of the words like they were nothing because to me they were. I simply sat there enjoying time out from the prison walls. I spent my time looking around the courtroom and enjoying a padded chair.

It was so comfortable. The last time I had sat in a chair so nice was when I was free. I was completely used to metal and concrete. Even my bunk at home was a hard rubber mat. The courthouse wasn't exciting. It was bland and boring like most were but it was still better than an ocean of grey. Eventually, I quit daydreaming and focused on the hearing.

The judge had listened to Mrs. Gartner's opening and once she finished he gave the floor to my attorney. This time, I enjoyed how differently it went. "Your Honor, I feel it is time we play the video for you to see." The prosecutor objected but the judge allowed the video anyway.

I actually enjoyed watching the judge's face as he watched. I could see his sympathy growing with every word the detective said. When it got to the part about the murder weapon, my attorney walked up and gave the evidence to the judge along with forensic evidence showing it was the finger prints of the detective and matching DNA of the victim.

I saw the judge glare at the prosecutor for even trying to oppose the case. The prosecutor didn't put up a lot of effort after that. She just let the case run its course. My attorney spoke at the closing.

"Your Honor, very valuable years have been stolen. My client paid a debt that he never deserved to pay. In all my years as an attorney, I have never felt so certain in the innocence of a defendant. The time is now. Let him free so he can use the rest of his years living out those dreams he thought he would never have the opportunity to fulfill."

My attorney sat down and the judge sat and thought for a moment. He opened his mouth as if he was going to speak and then closed it. He looked at me with so much sympathy. He managed to open his mouth and tell me, "It has been very rare in my life where I find myself speechless. This is one of those moments."

I was waiting for him to say due to some technicality he couldn't free me. I just wanted a chance to live a normal life. I clenched my teeth as I waited for him to make his ruling. "Mr. Cassidy, I find that the only option I truly feel would be correct is your immediate release. One day is too many in the event of true innocence. I am going to void the conviction with prejudice. This means that the state can no longer charge you with this crime. I wish you the best in the rest of your life. Mr. Cassidy, you're free to go." He smiled at me and said, "Court adjourned!" as he proudly pounded his gavel.

I started to cry. My attorney wrapped his arm around my shoulder as he was smiling. I stared at the desk in front of me. I couldn't believe that it was all over. I was so excited but at the same time, terrified. I turned and looked behind me but no one was there. I didn't have anyone anymore. My friends were in prison and my family had passed so long ago.

At that moment, I had to trust. God provides for the birds in the sky, He will provide for me as well. I decided to let God handle it and go from there. I walked out of the court house. I took a deep breath. It was my first fresh breath of air as a free man. Everything was beautiful. I hadn't realized how long it had been since I had seen a tree in real life. It was planted out front of the courthouse. I just had to touch it.

It was a beautiful day. There were flowers and birds. Mr. Barnes invited me to go get some food. Restaurants were everywhere and I couldn't decide what one to go to. My first meal as a free man was a burger and fries. It was simple and delicious. I couldn't explain how wonderful it was to have seasoned food. I was so used to bland foods I forgot what other food could taste like. Every bite was a gift.

We were both sitting and enjoying our food when a member from the local church approached us. He told me that he heard about the case and offered a bed to me. He showed me such generosity and hospitality. Most people wouldn't step out of their way to help a stranger but he did.

His name was Bill Warner. Over the next few months, I drove truck for his company. I worked and lived a normal life. Eventually, he helped me start the mill. Every day I woke up thankful to God for my freedom. Then God gave me another gift. It was Mr. Warner's daughter. She was a beautiful blonde-haired, blue-eyed girl with a matching passion for the Lord. We married shortly after meeting. Then God blessed us by sending our children into our life and we raised them to the best of our ability. God simply sent gift after gift.

Chapter 26

"WAIT, WHAT?" I ASKED DAD as he finished the story. "What ever happened to Matthew and Dom?" I had never been so interested in my dad's past before. I never knew he had been through so much. To go through what he went through and become the man he is was amazing to me.

"Well, both Matthew and Dom got out of prison. Once they were released, they never went back either. That is a battle for some inmates, but I told them before I was released that whatever put them in there would bring them back. Luckily, they listened and avoided that part of their life. It was easier for Matthew because he had a different mindset but they both got out and did very well."

I sat there thinking about all the loose ends in the story. I had so many questions I couldn't decide what to ask. I understood it is difficult for someone to sit down and give a detailed account of their entire life but I wanted to know everything. My dad was one of the most interesting people I had ever met.

"What about the riot? You saved everyone but you didn't get any recognition?" I asked.

Dad smiled at me. "I didn't do it for recognition. I did what I did because it was the right thing to do." I argued with him a little.

"But you were a hero and no one knew."

"That isn't true. God knew and to me that is all that matters."

I admired his humility. Most people want recognition and praise for saving someone's life.

"What about Gabe? What ever happened with that?" I asked.

Dad smiled once I brought up Gabe. "He is another story," he said.

"Well, we have nothing but time. What happened to him?" I asked.

"I only have my theories," he said.

"What? Did you ever go back for him?" Dad stood up before he answered my question.

"Want some hot chocolate?" He asked the girls. They sat up and walked with him into the kitchen. Dad never answered me. I was so curious about all the fine details of the story. Then the thought hit me. It would be a great birthday gift to find out what had happened to Gabe. We left that night saying I love you to each other. I had a plan in mind to find out what happened to my dad's best friend.

I took the next day off work. The twins went to school and Kelli ran errands. I told her what I was going to do and she said she would do some research of her own. I decided to take a two-hour drive to the capital. I wanted to make it an adventure and there was too much holding on the phone when I called any state department.

When I got there, it was slightly after ten. A very nice lady worked at the front desk and pointed me in the right direction. I walked through a couple hallways and found the right department.

"Hello, I'm trying to find out what happened to a man that was in prison with my dad." She gave me a confused look.

"He was in prison years ago and I'm trying to find out for him what happened to his cellmate," I said.

"Okay, I see. I could look him up on the computer and go from there," she responded.

"That would be awesome, thank you."

"Sir, what is his name?" She asked.

Then the thought hit me. I had no idea what his last name was. Dad only called him Gabe.

"Uh, his name was Gabe. I don't know his last name," I said. She laughed.

"Well that makes it a little difficult," she said sarcastically.

"He was my dad's cellmate. Could you look him up and find out who he lived with?" I asked.

"Yeah, I can do that but because the case is so old I might have to call the prison. They might not release any records but I will try. This sounds important to you."

"It is. Thank you so much," I said.

She nodded and told me to wait in the lobby as she walked off toward her office. I waited for hours. I didn't want to leave in case something came up. I was thinking about how dad must have felt. I waited a few hours, he waited for decades. I couldn't imagine what it was really like to go through what he went through.

Finally, I heard heels clicking against the hard floor. She walked up and said, "I found everything I could on Luke Cassidy. He was a very interesting man. He lived in prison during a very difficult time." I had waited so patiently. I just wanted her to get straight to the point.

"Anyway, I looked everywhere I could think of. The prison has records of your father in prison. It had his medical and disciplinary record but the prison has no record of Luke ever being housed with a Gabe or Gabriel, as far as I can find anyways. Are you sure he was his cellmate and not a friend housed somewhere else? Could he have possibly been one of his neighbors?" I shook my head.

"Dad said he was his cellmate. I am positive that he wasn't someone else." She sighed a little after my response.

"Well, I am sorry I don't have more information. I really wish I could do more to help."

"It's okay," I said.

I didn't have much more to say, so I left. I heard her high heels click back against the ground as she walked away in the opposite direction. I had so many questions running through my mind. I wanted answers and I was completely unsatisfied with the progress I had made. I walked out the door to my truck. I drove home constantly thinking about what the truth could actually be. Once

I entered back into town, the curiosity had overtaken me. I took a detour directly to dad's house.

I drove onto his driveway and parked by the house. I walked toward the door and peered into the window. He was relaxing on the couch. I knocked on the door and he came and opened it. He smiled when he saw me.

"What a pleasant surprise," he said.

"Dad, we need to talk."

I walked by him kind of rudely but my patience had run out. I needed to know the truth.

"Yeah, about what?" He asked.

"What really happened to Gabe? I drove to the capital and spent all day trying to figure out what happened to him."

Dad pointed toward the couch.

"Why don't you sit down?" He said.

I walked over and he followed me.

"I should have known you would do your research. You always were the curious type. Gabe is a very interesting subject. I did everything you have done and so much more to find him. The problem is I don't know if I can."

"What do you mean? He has to be somewhere," I said.

Dad nodded. "Yeah, I'm sure he is somewhere but I don't know where. I tried to find Gabe after I got out. I started by sending him letters. I kept receiving them back as if they were addressed wrongly. After a few weeks, I began to worry. I called the prison but they refused to release information. It got to the point where I had to get an attorney involved. I wanted to be able to visit my friend.

After several stressful months, I finally got a meeting with the warden to go back to the prison. When I got there, it seemed exactly as I left it. I didn't miss anything about it but it brought back many types of memories. I could picture my life as if I was still there. I would have been living my life just as before, stuck in the monotonous routine. It was torturous.

Anyway, when I entered the front gate of the prison, the warden was waiting for me. He had to escort me throughout the prison. We walked straight to my old cell and when I saw it, I was shocked. It didn't look the same. The room seemed smaller and there was only a single bunk. My first rational thought was they replaced the bunk but the warden assured me nothing had changed.

I didn't have any reason to believe that the warden would lie about that. I walked around the cell for a few short minutes. I had a unique feeling about the place. I was neither happy nor sad. I was in a blank place in between with not much emotion at all. I was just there.

It had been such a large part of my life so it still felt like home. I didn't want to move back but some things I missed. It was so quiet and the concrete radiated the coolness of the air off the walls. It was comfortable to me. That tends to happen when you spend a majority of your life somewhere.

I wiped my hand over the metal desk to see how it felt. The chill ran from my knuckles all the way up my arm. At that point, I was overwhelmed with how thankful I was to not have to live there anymore. I was so happy that when I left there I would be able to sit on a couch with cushions and comfort.

I turned back to the warden. I got straight to the point and bluntly asked him, "Where is Gabe?" At that point he spoke into his radio, "Send him." My first instinct told me to rejoice. They had Gabe and I was going to be able to see him.

A few minutes later, a man walked up. He was a doctor, a psychologist to be exact. He worked for the prison and dealt primarily with the extremely mentally ill. He spoke to me explaining all his credentials and then said what he was there to say.

He told me that sometimes, men in my type of situation see things that might not actually be there. He explained the possibility that the stress had made me design a friend from my conscious. He went on talking about that for a while and I got to the point where I was becoming angry. I didn't go there for a doctor's appointment,

I went to see Gabe. He was being as polite as he could in calling me crazy but I didn't care. It wasn't even a possibility to me that Gabe was a hallucination. He was too real to be fake.

The doctor handed the warden a manila file folder. He opened it and very seriously told me that I never had a cell mate. He showed me my entire inmate file. I glanced past my disciplinary records. I didn't care to be reminded of my poor choices. Then the warden showed me a piece of paper titled Housing Arrangements.

It stated my entry and exit date. Then my cell, J-47, but what it said next shocked me. It said one word, solitary. It didn't make any sense to me. I wasn't by myself, I was with Gabe. He was real. I had too many memories of him. Our conversations were too deep to be a figment of my imagination. I had a look of shock on my face. I looked up at the warden and he apologized to me.

I couldn't make a decision on what was true. I knew what I saw. I replayed all the memories in my mind. I could see him smiling his bright white smile. Out of all the memories I had, that was the first to come to mind. He was a genuinely happy person. I could see his face as I spoke. He listened and cared about everything I had to say. He was too important in my life for me to believe he didn't exist.

I was at the point where I didn't want to hear any more about a make believe friend. I decided it would be good judgment to leave. I wanted to take one last look through my cell to say goodbye. I was ready to leave those chapters of my life behind. I walked in and glanced around at the floor and walls. I turned around to walk out and then I saw it.

At that moment, I felt closer to God than I had ever felt before. It was a moment of clarity and I knew the truth. I wasn't crazy and Gabe wasn't a figment of my imagination. I started to cry as I looked at the painted white cross just above my doorway. It was still there exactly the way I left it. I remembered watching Gabe paint it.

My tears were tears of joy. I didn't take long looking up at the cross. My mind was racing too fast for me to stay there. I wanted to get away to think. I left the prison, walking out for the last time.

Once I got out to my car, I began to bawl uncontrollably. I couldn't keep it together. My theory was real, even though it was hard to believe. God loved me so much he sent an angel to be by my side. Through thick and thin he was always there. I had loved God and prayed to Him, but I never thought He would bless me like He did. I was humbled and thankful.

I was bawling and thinking. The more I thought about what happened, the more my bawl transformed into a laugh. It was a mixture of crying and laughing, but it was all out of joy. I prayed in my car, "Thank you, Jesus." I drove home and went on with the rest of my life not speaking much about it. I was reassured over and over again that Gabe was an angel. It was the small things that told me, but I still paid enough attention to notice."

Chapter 27

THE PHONE RANG IN THE middle of the night. I woke up suddenly because the unusualness of a phone call at three in the morning. I sat up and grabbed my phone off my bedside table. I opened the phone and spoke in a sleepy tone.

"Hello?"

"Hello, is this Jace Cassidy? I have this phone number down as an emergency reference for your father." I was instantly awake as my heart started to beat harder. I had a surge of worry cross my mind.

"Yeah, this is. What happened?" I asked.

"It's about your dad. He is in the hospital. He called an ambulance after he coughed up blood and it's very serious. We need you to come to the hospital." I didn't hesitate for a second.

"Okay," I said as I hung up the phone. I told Kelli everything I knew as I put on my clothes. She told me that she would meet me there.

I ran to my truck and sped to the hospital. Once I got there, I parked and bolted through the sliding glass doors. I ran up to the lady at the front desk.

"Where is Luke Cassidy? He is my father and I just got a call he is here in critical condition." She looked at her computer screen then pointed down the hall.

"Room 238," She said.

I ran all the way there. I glanced past the doors looking at all the numbers growing toward 238. I got to his door and took a deep breath as I entered the room. A nurse was standing by his side checking his vitals. She looked at me and told me he was alive. He wasn't conscious when I walked up next to his bed. The nurse smiled at me and said, "I'll give you some space."

I didn't say anything. I just grabbed a chair and pulled it up next to him. I watched him sleep for a few minutes. I was thinking about my entire life. I never wanted to envision my life without dad around. I became more emotional after I thought about him dying. I would miss him.

After a few minutes, I started to talk to him. I didn't know what to talk about so I just spoke. I started by talking about how much he meant to me. He was one of the most important people in my life. I wanted him to be around forever. I wasn't ready for him to go. I was crying while I spoke. I pulled the chair close and held onto his hand. I leaned over onto his bed and listened to his heart beating. I laid there counting his heartbeats until I fell asleep.

I woke up to someone shaking my shoulder. Dad was sitting up in his bed smiling down at me.

"Rise and shine," he said. I sat up and lunged to give him a hug. He embraced me.

"How are you feeling?" I asked. He gave me a smirk.

"I've had worse days," he said with a laugh.

Kate and her husband walked into the hospital room. She had a vase of flowers that she set by the window.

"Good morning," she said with a smile.

We all started in on a conversation apart from dad's health. After about an hour, a doctor walked in. He talked to Kate's husband for a second and then we walked out to talk to him. Dad had a lot of energy and seemed to be fine.

"So, what's the word?" I asked the doctor.

"Well, it isn't good. He may seem okay but the cancer has spread over the entirety of his lungs. He may make you believe he is okay but my recommendation is to put him in hospice care. Honestly, it is a medical miracle that he is alive today."

I heard what the doctor had to say but it didn't quite register. The only word that had any meaning to me was miracle. I stood there day dreaming. My dad's life itself was a miracle. His patience and perseverance was inspiring. He was living on time he wasn't supposed to have, according to the doctor anyway, and yet there he was on a hospital bed, smiling and happy.

It really is all about perception. Some men have everything the world has to offer but in all reality they have nothing. And some men with nothing could actually have everything. I chimed back into the conversation.

"So what's the next step?" I asked.

"With your permission, I believe we should put him into hospice. He will have full-time care and you can still visit at any time. I believe that would be the best option." Kate's husband agreed so I took their advice.

The next day, I went to the hospice home to check on dad. It was a great facility from the looks of it. Dad had oxygen tubes in his nostrils when I saw him.

He chuckled, "Like the new look?"

"Yeah, you can make anything look good," I said to boost his ego.

His energy seemed so normal I felt that he didn't need to be there but little things showed me he was actually in pain. I knew he was putting up a front so I wouldn't worry. It showed his true character. He was the one on his deathbed and his only care was that I wouldn't worry. I loved his selflessness. I loved him.

A few minutes after I got there, Kelli walked in with the twins. His face lit up once he saw them.

"Grandpa!" They yelled. They were smiling when they ran and jumped up on his bed.

"How are my babies?" He asked.

"Good," they replied with a bashful tone.

"We miss you," Hope said. Faith nodded in agreement. Dad started to show his emotion. I knew he was hurting from the thought of leaving us behind but at the same time he was excited to finally go home. Death is the most bittersweet moment man can experience.

We visited dad every day. His health started to become less consistent. Some days he seemed healthy as ever and others I could see the toll the cancer took on him. It was really tough on everybody but we all came together as a family to ensure dad was as comfortable as possible.

I remember his last day so clearly. It was a Thursday. I went and saw dad after work. When I got there, he was vibrant and full of life. It was like every other visit we had over the last few weeks.

We talked for a few hours about everything we could think of. I definitely was my father's son. Our opinions on nearly every issue were identical. I had always been close with my dad but sitting down having a close conversation made me feel even closer. I cherished the moments of simply talking to him.

The phone rang in the middle of the night. I turned over in my bed and looked at the clock. It read 3:29 a.m. I answered my cell phone. It was the nurse from hospice on the other end of the line.

"Your father has passed," she said softly. I slowly sat up in bed. I had dreaded to hear those words my entire life. My first thought was it can't be true.

"What do you mean? He was feeling great this afternoon," I said.

"I'm sorry," she replied.

I sat back down on my bed. Kelli was awake by then and put her hand on my shoulder. I sighed deeply and the tears started to roll down my cheek. I told the nurse, "I will be right there," and hung up the phone.

I leaned back on the bed and stared at the ceiling. It was my first experience without my dad in my life and I didn't want to believe it was true. Kelli gave me a few minutes to breath before she asked, "Are you okay?"

"Yeah," I lied.

The truth was I was deeply hurt. I didn't want to imagine my life without him but it was my only option. I loved my father and would miss him. I did the most important thing my dad had taught me in times of trouble. I prayed.

"Father, I knew one day you would take dad. Thank you so much for the blessing of his life and the years you gave us. Please comfort my family. You know how much he meant to us and it will be hard to adapt to life without him. Jesus, please don't leave or forsake me. In Jesus's name I pray, Amen."

Three days had passed before we had the funeral. Kate made a video collage from all our family photos. I started to cry about ten seconds in. The music and emotion of everything made it too difficult to keep my composure. A few photos made me smile, even laugh, but the thought of knowing he was gone always made me cry. At least in the photos, I could see the happiness in his face.

We closed the ceremony with me saying a few words. I knew it would be hard to keep from crying so I kept the speaking to a minimum. "Luke Cassidy was a loved man. He helped a lot of people. Even to those whose entire experience with him lasted only a few minutes, he still made an impact. He was a gentleman and a disciple. I have no doubt that he is finally home. I know he is happy and laughing. He is finally at peace." I looked down at the twins next to Kelli. That was when the tears started to roll in quite heavily.

I wanted them to have grandparents around but life is out of man's control. I looked back out to the masses of people that attended dad's funeral. Dad completed his goal. He made a dent on the world. He walked the road that God laid out for him. He was one of the few who were loved both deeply and widely.

After I spoke, we all headed to the cemetery to bury him. We pulled up to the cemetery and I stepped out of my truck. I took a deep breath and looked up to the sky. I asked God for strength because I knew I had run out. I took a step onto the freshly cut grass but had to stop because my legs refused to move. I squatted down to my heels and prayed again.

I felt a rush of comfort tell me to be patient. I listened even though it was hard. I reached my hand down to the grass and felt its dampness. The coolness of the grass distracted me from the fear of life without dad. I told myself at that moment I needed to show strength for my family.

We decided to lay dad to rest right next to mom. We knew he would have wanted that. I tried to listen to the pastor as we lowered his beautiful oak casket into the grave. I was distracted by all the emotions crossing my mind. Then my focus turned to the yellow flowers surrounding the grave site. I felt a few tears stroll down my cheek when I looked over at a butterfly landing on one of the flowers. It made me hurt for my kids. The funeral ended and I took a moment to say my final goodbye.

The twins and Kelli left for the truck. I didn't take long and I started to head for the truck too. I was stopped by the hospice nurse that took care of dad in his last days. I was happy that she had made it to his funeral. It showed how easily he was loved.

"Your dad was a good man," she said.

"Yeah, he was," I replied.

"I wanted to stop you and tell you about his finally minutes on earth. I want you to take comfort in knowing he died peacefully."

"Well, thank you," I replied.

"But when your dad died, I had a unique experience that I can't explain. He was murmuring at me. It sounded faint and I couldn't quite understand him. At first I thought he was trying to say Gail. I couldn't make it out for a while but he finally spoke clearly enough for me to understand him. Does the name Gabriel have any meaning to you?"

"Yeah it does, why?" I replied curiously.

"Well, right before he died, he faintly called out, 'Gabriel, Gabriel' and reached out his arm. I turned to see what he was looking at but nothing was there. And in his last breath he softly spoke, 'I knew you were real.' I didn't see anything and I don't know what it means, but I thought you should know."

She didn't know the impact of what she had just told me but I did. I smiled and looked up toward heaven. My grin widened as I thought to myself, *God will never leave or forsake me."*

If your heart has been touched in a way that makes you feel it is time to accept Jesus Christ as your Lord and Savior, then the time is now. If you know in your core that this is what you want to do, then pray with me.

"Father, I acknowledge I am a sinner. I accept your gift of eternal salvation. I proclaim Jesus is Lord and He died on the cross for my sins. In Jesus's name I pray. Amen."

It is as simple as that. If you spoke those words and believed them with all your heart then welcome to Christianity, you are now born again. Remember that God loves you and He always has. Live a life of faith and be in God's word. Abundance will fill your soul.

NKJV John 3:16, "For God so loved the world he gave his only begotten Son, that whoever believes in Him should not perish but have everlasting life."

About the Author

J.M. Vierstra was born in southern Idaho and grew up on a dairy farm. He grew up with Christian roots and leaned on that foundation through his adversity and liberty. Whether he was on top of the mountain or at the bottom, his trust in Christ didn't waver. He found comfort in the word of God and support of his family.

He has had many experiences in his first twenty years of life. He has experienced both triumph and failure. His greatest goal is to send a message that God loves us all and is always by our side. That is why he wrote this book in the first place. He was looking for a way to reach out to those who were searching. He wanted to inform those with an overwhelming emptiness inside themselves that they need Christ to fill that void. Nothing else can fulfill you or give you that contentment.

In the end, the biggest message is like that in the Bible. Love one another like Christ loves you. The greatest gift is giving itself. Give your time and love to everyone around you. Live a life of generosity and grace. In the end, all we have is our memories. Make those memories worth reflecting on.

"Under The Red Oak Tree" is a thoughtfully written and thought provoking story at the intersection of the justice system and human experience. The author accurately portrays life within prison walls and offers a reminder that even within the darkest struggles of life, the hope of the gospel remains a light that transcends the bleakest circumstances. This story reminds us that the presence of God is uncompromisingly dependable since no one is ever disqualified from redemption and grace.

Rev. Brian Vriesman